Why Me?

"Mom!" Sam said to her mother. "Dad says I can't date."

"You have a date?" her mother asked.

"Yeah, and he's a cute guy, but now Dad says I can't," Sam spoke in an anxious rush. This couldn't be happening. She'd finally gotten a date and now she couldn't go! "Mom, I can go, can't I?"

Mrs. O'Neill turned to her husband. "Dan, maybe you should think about—"

"I've thought about nothing else all day," he replied. "We let Greta date too young, and we're not making the same mistake with Sam. She's not dating until she's sixteen. And then I'll *think* about it!"

"That's not fair, Dad," cried Sam. "I'm not Greta. I'm totally dif—"

"I said no!" Mr. O'Neill exploded. "And that's final!"

**Look for these other books in the
SITTING PRETTY series:**

SITTING PRETTY
BOY TROUBLE

by Suzanne Weyn

Troll Associates

Library of Congress Cataloging-in-Publication Data

Weyn, Suzanne.
  Boy trouble / by Suzanne Weyn; illustrated by Joel Iskowitz.
      p.   cm. (Sitting pretty; #5)
    Summary: Wanting to start dating at the same time as her two best
  friends, ninth-grader Sam begins secretly seeing the handsome Kyle
  Jameson, even though her father has forbidden her to date until she
  is sixteen.
    ISBN 0-8167-2011-8 (lib. bdg.)   ISBN 0-8167-2012-6 (pbk.)
    [1. Dating (Social customs)—Fiction.]   I. Iskowitz, Joel, ill.
  II. Title.   III. Series: Weyn, Suzanne. Sitting pretty; #5.
  PZ7.W539Bo   1991
  [Fic]—dc20   90-11142

A TROLL BOOK, published by Troll Associates,
Mahwah, NJ 07430

Printed in the United States of America.

10   9   8   7   6   5   4   3   2   1

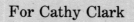

For Cathy Clark

Chapter One

Sam O'Neill looked down at little Courtney Rutherford. The four-year-old was on her back, arms flailing and legs kicking furiously. Two long brown braids lashed about her beet-red face as she shook her head and screamed.

"I give up!" cried Sam's friend, Liza Velez, who stood beside Sam at the Palm Pavilion Hotel's pool deck. "I don't know what to do. I can't get her to stop."

Sam noticed that the people lounging around the pool were staring at them. They looked annoyed, as if Sam and Liza were the ones making all the noise.

Their friend Chris Brown stood in the water minding three-year-old Howie and six-year-old Esmee, who were playing in the shallow end of the pool. "What, exactly, is bugging Courtney now?" she asked.

"She wants to wear her sneakers into the pool and I told her she couldn't," Liza explained. Then she crouched down beside the little girl. "Come on, Courtney, cut it out. Please. Pretty please," she begged.

Courtney responded to Liza's plea by screaming even louder.

"Sam, do something!" Liza pleaded.

Sam knelt down by the screaming girl. In the two and a half months that she'd been a staff baby sitter at the Palm Pavilion Hotel, she'd dealt with a number of temper tantrums. She knew that the best approach was to attempt to distract the child. That worked most of the time.

"Courtney," Sam said sweetly.

Courtney continued to wail.

"Courtney," Sam repeated more sternly. This time she grabbed the girl's legs and held them. That got Courtney's attention.

"Let me go! Let me go!" Courtney screamed, but Sam held on. After a few minutes, Courtney lay there on the cement, panting and red-faced.

"Do you know how to play sea horse?" Sam asked Courtney.

Suspiciously, Courtney shook her head no.

"I'll be the sea horse and you can ride on my back in the pool," Sam explained.

Courtney's eyes lit up enthusiastically. "Okay," she said, sitting up and rubbing the tears from her eyes.

"Come on, take off your sneakers and let's go into the pool," Sam instructed.

Courtney seemed to forget all about wanting to wear her red sneakers into the water. She pulled them off and got to her feet. "I'm ready."

"You're amazing," Liza told Sam. "I don't know how you do it."

Sam smiled. "That was just luck."

"Don't be so modest," said Chris. "You're really good with kids. Even B-R-A-T-S like you-know-who."

"Thanks," Sam replied. She knew Chris was right. She did seem to have an ability with kids. She didn't know why. Maybe it was just because she liked them a lot. Even a kid like Courtney didn't bother her—well, not that much.

Once they were in the pool, Courtney climbed onto Sam's back and grabbed Sam's long blond ponytail. "No, hold me around the neck," Sam corrected the girl. Courtney did as she said, and Sam sank down into the water up to her shoulders.

"I'll watch Howie while you take Courtney," Liza offered. That afternoon when the girls reported to work, Courtney had been assigned to Liza's care. Sam was in charge of Howie and Chris had been told to take care of Esmee.

"Okay," Sam answered, swimming in circles with Courtney on her back. "I don't think anyone will care if we switch."

Liza pulled her long dark hair back into a loose braid. "You're a pal," she said. She took a beach ball from the side of the pool and tossed it to Howie. "Comin' at ya, Howie," she called. "Catch!"

Liza threw the ball back and forth with Howie. Chris was showing Esmee how to float and Sam continued to

3

swim with Courtney. For the moment, things were peaceful.

Sam let her thoughts wander as she swam, and she began to think about school. It was the first year of high school for Chris, Liza and Sam. The small town of Bonita Beach had only one high school, and it wasn't very big. Still, the girls were nervous and excited about being freshmen.

"I think I'm going to try out for the school gymnastics team," Sam told her friends as she moved through the water. "I saw a notice for tryouts on the gym bulletin board."

"Are you interested in gymnastics?" asked Chris, looking up from the floating Esmee.

"Are you kidding?" Liza laughed. "Sam is interested in any sport that you can name. You should know that, Chris."

"I know she's a super-jock. I just never thought she was that excited about gymnastics," Chris replied, brushing a piece of her newly bleached blond hair from her eyes.

"I never liked it that much when we did it in gym," Sam admitted, "although I didn't find it too difficult. But the gymnastic events in the last Olympics were really cool. It made me want to try. Wouldn't it be great to be in the Olympics?"

"Wow! You're thinking big," Liza noted admiringly.

"The notice at school said there would be two practices before the tryouts," Sam continued. "That's good, because I haven't done anything since last year."

"How are you going to fit everything in?" asked Chris. "With school and working, you're already pretty busy."

"I know," said Sam. "But I'll manage somehow."

Sam knew it wouldn't be easy to cram another event into her schedule; her job at the Palm Pavilion already took up a lot of her free time. But the thought of competing in a new sport was exciting.

"Want to swim into the deep water?" Sam asked Courtney.

"Yeah!" the girl cried happily.

Sam ventured out into the middle of the pool. The water wasn't over her head, but it would seem deep to little Courtney. Sam was a strong, confident swimmer and she planned to take Lifeguard Training when she was sixteen. She hoped that one day, she'd be hired as a lifeguard at the Palm.

In the summer, Sam, Chris and Liza had worked almost every day at the posh hotel that was located on the outskirts of Bonita Beach. The majestic hotel—with its soft pink stucco walls and crisp white canopies—was at the end of a long country road dense with palms and other tropical foliage. If you didn't know where it was, you might never find it.

But movie stars, business tycoons and millionaires *did* know where it was. They found the palatial hotel, nestled in a secluded spot beside the crystal blue ocean, there at the end of southern Florida. And they flocked to it, expecting the ultimate in privacy and luxury.

Now that school had started, the girls worked a few days each week in the afternoon and Saturdays. Sam's parents had told her she could keep working as long as she kept her grades up. It wouldn't be a snap; Sam had to work for her grades. But she was determined to do it all—school, work and now gymnastics.

"No more sea horse," Courtney told Sam. "I'm tired of holding on."

"Okay, kiddo," said Sam. "I'll swim you over to the shallow end."

When Sam let Courtney slide from her back at the shallow end of the pool, she saw that Chris and Liza were sitting on the edge, deep in conversation. From their expressions she could tell that they were worried about something.

"What's up?" she asked, wading over to where they sat.

"Oh, nothing," said Liza, sounding evasive.

Sam frowned. This was strange. It wasn't like her two best friends to keep a secret from her.

"I know something's got you guys bugged. I can see it on your faces," she pressed. "Tell me."

Chris and Liza exchanged guilty glances.

"It's this hair, " said Chris, holding out a strand of her blond hair. "The roots are coming in and it looks horrible. I wish I'd never bleached it. I want to let my own color grow back. But I don't want to be walking around with half-blond and half-reddish hair. It's bad enough I have this extra ten pounds that I can never seem to lose, now I have this weird hair to deal with, too."

Sam studied Chris's chin-length hair. It was looking pretty bad. Her once-shiny, strawberry-blond color was now a dull, dried-out blond. And the roots were notice-able. "We can ask Greta," she suggested. Sam's older sister was always bleaching her hair. She'd know what to do.

"Good idea," agreed Chris.

Something was still wrong. Sam could feel it. There was something else besides Chris's hair that was bothering them. "Are you sure there's nothing else the matter?" she asked.

Once again, Liza and Chris looked at each other, concern in their eyes. Then they looked back to Sam and sighed.

"Okay," said Liza. "We were discussing how to tell you something without hurting your feelings."

"What?" Sam asked with a nervous laugh. "Do I have bad breath?"

"No," Liza said, not smiling. Her long, thin legs dangled into the water. She studied her red toenails a moment. "You explain it, Chris," she said, turning to her friend.

"What is it?" Sam cried, anxious to know what this awful news could be.

Chris sighed again. "I'm just going to come out and say it, okay?"

Sam felt her heart speed up a little. Suddenly she wasn't so sure she wanted to hear this. "Go ahead," she said bravely.

"Bruce asked me to go to the movies with him this Saturday," Chris began.

"And Eddie asked me to go to the same movie," Liza

7

added. "The guys thought it would be fun to sort of double date."

Sam stared at them blankly, letting their words soak in. "But I thought *we* were going to go to the movies together Saturday."

"That's the problem," said Chris glumly.

Chapter Two

Sam handed Courtney a hot dog from Sal's Snack Bar. The little girl hadn't even asked for one, but Sam needed an excuse to get away from Chris and Liza for a moment. She didn't want them to see that their news had bothered her.

They had invited her to come along on their double date. But, of course, she'd said no. Tagging along on their date would be *too* embarrassing.

Instead, she'd forced herself to smile and say that it was okay, she understood. The three of them could go to the movies together anytime.

But was it really okay? Sam tried to sort out her true feelings as she unwrapped a straw and stuck it into Courtney's box of juice.

So many feelings were jumbled up inside her right now. *Am I angry?* she asked herself. *Yes, definitely. But do I have a right to be?* She wasn't sure.

Yes, I do have a right to be angry, she decided after a

moment. *They have some nerve, dumping me because two boys come along.*

Then she remembered that they hadn't dumped her. They'd invited her along. It was the same as being dumped, though. They knew she wouldn't come. They should have told the boys they were busy!

Sam sighed. Chris had been dying to go out with Bruce all summer. Now that he'd finally asked her, could Sam really expect Chris not to go? *What kind of friend does that make me?* she reproached herself.

"All done," Courtney chirped, smiling at Sam with a mustard-smeared mouth.

Sam smiled back. This kid wasn't really so bad. Sam realized that she even liked her. Courtney was strong-willed—but so was Sam. Maybe that was why Sam could manage her so well.

"I want to swim more," Courtney told Sam.

"All right." Sam took the girl's hand and walked back to the pool area. Liza and Chris were playing with their kids. They stopped when they saw Sam approach. "Go play with Howie," Sam told Courtney.

"Chris and I have been talking," said Liza, joining Sam on the wide steps leading into the pool. "What if we got one of Eddie and Bruce's friends to take you out?"

"A blind date?" cried Sam. "No way!"

"Okay, then," said Liza. "We three can still go out together on Saturday. We'll just tell Bruce and Eddie we'll see them on Sunday."

Part of Sam wanted to agree to this plan. She couldn't do it, though. For one thing, the look on Chris's face told

Sam that it would kill her not to go out on Saturday after waiting so long. Besides, the evening at the movies was already spoiled for Sam. What fun would it be if she knew her friends would rather be there with Bruce and Eddie?

"No, you guys go," Sam said.

"You don't mind?" asked Chris.

"I do mind," Sam admitted honestly. "But I might as well get used to it. Bruce and Eddie are best friends. And you two are friends. It's natural that you're going to want to do stuff together."

She hadn't expected a lump to form in her throat as she said these words. She hated lumps in her throat. They meant that tears were just around the corner.

What's the matter with me? she scolded herself, looking away in case the tears did come. She didn't want to cry here in the pool, in front of the kids and everyone.

The problem was that she was suddenly afraid of being left out. The three of them had been doing everything together ever since grammar school. Now that was changing. And she was the one who might be left alone without her two best friends. All because she didn't have a stupid old boyfriend!

"Don't cry," said Liza, gently touching her arm.

"I'm not crying!" Sam snapped in a cracked voice.

Sam stared up at the sky. *I feel so dumb*, she thought. In a moment the lump and the tingle of threatening tears had gone.

"We're not going to be doing every single thing with Bruce and Eddie," said Chris in a consoling voice.

"You're sure?" asked Sam.

"Positive," Liza assured her.

"Hey, Bruce might not even like me after this date," Chris volunteered cheerfully. "Who knows? Maybe he'll think I'm a total nerd or something."

Sam smiled despite herself. It was nice of Chris to suggest the worst just to make her feel better. "You're not a nerd, Chris," said Sam.

"I know I'm not," replied Chris. "But Bruce might think it. You know how boys can be."

"No, I don't really know," said Sam glumly. "That's the problem. If I had a boyfriend, the three of us could go out together."

"We can find you one," Liza suggested. "They're not that hard to get."

"Not hard for you," said Sam. "Boys always like you." Sam knew that ever since sixth grade boys had been passing Liza notes and asking her to go steady. They seemed to like Liza's high spirits and outspoken manner.

Plus, Sam considered, Liza was very pretty—with her big dark eyes, long legs and slim figure. Sam knew she was far from ugly, herself. People had even called her cute. But no boy had ever asked her out.

"Do you think something's the matter with me?" she asked Chris and Liza. "How come boys aren't interested?"

"Nothing's the matter with you!" Chris spoke up loyally. "You're pretty and you're nice. You have a good personality. You're good at sports."

"Could that be turning guys off?" asked Sam. "Do I seem too—you know—jockish?"

"Maybe to some boys," Liza said frankly. "But not all. Lots of sporty-type girls have boyfriends."

"Then what is it?" Sam asked despairingly.

"You'll find somebody," Chris said. "There's not anybody around that you like, is there?"

"No," said Sam.

"That could be part of it," Liza suggested. "If you like a boy first, he can tell. That gives him the courage to ask you out. You have to sort of give them some encouragement."

"I can't flirt," said Sam. "I'd feel like a jerk."

"You have to try!" Liza said.

"I know how Sam feels," Chris said. "I didn't flirt with Bruce, I only—"

"Oh, you did too flirt with Bruce!" Liza cut her off. "You only bought about three tons of vegetables for our party so that Bruce could help you chop them up for the veggie plate."

"That's not flirting," Chris replied. "It's—it's scheming and plotting—but it is *not* flirting."

"Call it whatever you like!" Liza exploded. "You still didn't sit around and wait for Bruce to come to you. You took action. You even bleached your hair so he'd notice you!"

Chris pulled a strand of blond hair in front of her green eyes. "Now I wish I hadn't, though. It looks so horrible."

"That's not the point!" cried Liza, exasperated. "You did something to get Bruce and you got him."

"Hold on, hold on," said Sam. "Bruce wasn't any old guy. Chris was already nuts about him. I don't have anybody I feel that way about."

"Well, maybe you're just not looking," Liza said sulkily.

"Don't be mad at me because I don't have a boyfriend," Sam said with an insulted air.

"I wish you would get one. Then this problem would go away," Liza said. "You don't know. I've hardly even slept the last two nights, I was so worried about how you'd feel about this Saturday."

"Oh, excuse me," said Sam sarcastically. "Now it's my fault."

"It's not anybody's fault," Chris said calmly. "We'll figure it all out somehow. Why don't you come with us this Saturday? You know Bruce and Eddie. And they like you."

"Thanks but no thanks," Sam answered.

Their conversation was cut off by a howl from little Howie. Courtney was holding his toy boat over his head and the toddler was jumping for it, screaming all the while.

"It's all right, Howie," said Chris, wading toward the boy. "Help is on its way."

Sam checked her black waterproof watch. "It's five. We might as well start getting these kids dried off and back to the lobby." They were due to return the children to their parents by five-thirty. Experience had taught them that it took a half-hour for the kids to find their towels, thongs, dry off and then dillydally on their way back up to the hotel lobby.

After getting out of the pool and drying herself, Courtney refused to put her sneakers back on. "No! No! No sneakers," she shouted.

"This kid is unbelievable," Liza muttered.

"Courtney," Sam spoke to the girl. "I don't want you to put your sneakers on." She scooped up the small sneakers. "You can't put on your sneakers."

"I want to wear my sneakers!" cried Courtney.

Sam knelt and held out the sneakers. "All right, I'll help you get them on."

"You're amazing. Simply amazing," Liza said.

When the kids were ready, the girls walked with them back to the hotel. As they neared the sliding glass doors that led into the lobby, Liza grabbed Sam's arm.

"Who's that hunk over there stacking beach chairs?" she asked.

"I don't know," said Sam, looking at the tall, muscular boy who was working several yards away. "I've never seen him before."

"There's a whole bunch of new people now because the college kids went back to school," said Chris.

"Well, I know one thing," said Liza. "Before we leave here today, we're going to find out *everything* about him!"

Chapter Three

The girls returned the kids to their parents and then punched out on the hotel time clock. Liza rushed Sam and Chris as they changed from their bathing suits into their shorts and official Palm Pavilion polo shirts. "We have to decide if Sam is interested in this new guy before someone else snaps him up," Liza said, hurrying Sam and Chris back out to the pool area.

"Good, he's still there," said Liza, spotting the boy over by the pool.

"How are you going to meet him?" asked Sam.

"No problem," Liza answered confidently. "We work here. He works here. We're just being friendly."

"I don't know," Chris said doubtfully. Liza didn't even hear her. She was already walking up to the handsome boy as if she represented an official welcoming committee. Sam and Chris followed more timidly, several paces behind.

By the time they caught up to her, Liza was getting

directly to the heart of the matter, finding out who this boy was and where he came from. "Kyle Jameson, meet Sam O'Neill and Chris Brown, my two very best friends," she introduced them.

"Pleased to meet you," he said.

"You're new in Bonita Beach, aren't you?" Liza said to the tall, brown-haired boy.

He looked at her with light blue eyes. His cheekbones were wide and high. His nose was straight and angular. "How can you tell I'm new?"

"How can I tell?" Liza laughed, poking Sam and Chris. "Very humorous. You're quite witty, aren't you?"

Sam tried not to wince. Sometimes Liza came on a little too strong when she was trying to be charming. Too strong for Sam, anyway. But boys seemed to love it.

"No, seriously, I'm interested," said Kyle. "How did you know I just moved here?"

"Bonita Beach is a pretty small town," Chris explained. "We sort of know everyone under eighteen, at least by sight."

"Unless you go to private school and live over in the Heights—we know you." Liza concluded proudly.

"The Heights?" asked Kyle.

"That's the fancy part of Bonita Beach," Sam told him.

"No. I suppose my house is in plain old Bonita Beach," he said. "We just moved to Heron Drive."

"Yes, Heron Drive is definitely not swanky," Liza agreed.

"Liza!" Chris scolded, giving Liza a small shove.

"I wasn't being rude," Liza defended herself. "None of us lives in the Heights. It's no big deal."

"How come we haven't seen you in school?" Sam asked, trying to change the subject.

"I just started today. I'm a senior," he replied, running his hand along the top of his closely cropped hair. As he spoke to Sam, he seemed to be studying her. "We only moved in last Wednesday."

"And you got a job that fast?" Chris questioned.

"Mr. Parker told me he just happened to have a spot open," he said, referring to the hotel's demanding manager.

"What do you think of old prune-face Parker?" asked Liza.

"Mr. Parker isn't that horrible," said Sam before Kyle could answer. "He's let us get away with a lot of things that someone else might have fired us for."

"And he did adjust our hours so that we could work after school and on Saturday now that summer is over," added Chris. "He didn't have to do that."

"I suppose," Liza conceded. "Still, you have to admit he's a pain."

"He *is* a pain sometimes," Chris agreed.

"Uh-oh," said Liza, looking up toward the hotel. "Speaking of Parker, he's headed this way. You'd better get back to stacking beach chairs, Kyle. And try to look like you're kicking up a sweat. That will impress Parker. He loves hard workers."

"There are no idlers at the Palm Pavilion," Chris

joked, repeating the manager's favorite saying in her best Mr. Parker imitation.

"It's all right," said Kyle. "I'm not worried about him."

"Well, we are," said Chris hurriedly. "So we're getting out of here before he blames us for distracting you."

"You're right," Liza agreed. "*Adios*," she told Kyle quickly.

"So long," he said. Sam noticed that although he was speaking to them all, he was staring at her. In fact, he hadn't taken his eyes off her from the moment they were introduced.

"Bye," Sam said, feeling uncomfortable under the scrutiny of his intense gaze.

On their way back to the hotel, they had to pass Mr. Parker. As always, the tall, pencil-thin man seemed to be in a great hurry and walked with a smart clip to his step. He was dressed in his usual attire: Bermuda shorts belted too high at the waist; a cotton shirt, buttoned up to the neck; socks and sandals. Strands of thin hair were combed across the top of his balding head to give the illusion of more hair.

"Ladies," he greeted the girls as they passed by.

"Hello, Mr. Parker," they replied in one voice.

He eyed them sharply, as if sure they were up to no good. In the months that they'd worked for him, the girls had had more than one run-in with Mr. Parker. They just couldn't seem to keep track of his many rules.

He raised an arched brow, a sure sign that he had detected some infraction of the rules. "Miss Brown," he said. "Do we own an iron?"

"Do *we*?" Chris repeated, confused. "I don't know, sir. I'm not sure what you mean."

Mr. Parker's nostrils flared with irritation. "I was using *we* as a figure of speech. I want to see some creases in those shorts tomorrow. Burn those rumpled things you're wearing if you have to. Do you hear me?"

"Yes, sir," Chris answered.

"The Palm Pavilion staff has to look neat and professional," he said. Without another word, he walked off into the pool area.

"Boy, that guy doesn't even want you to get your clothes wrinkled while you work," Chris complained, smoothing her shorts. "I don't think I look that bad."

"Forget it," said Liza as the girls continued on their way up to the hotel. "You know Parker. Everything has to be perfect."

"What did you think of Kyle?" asked Sam.

"Cute but boring," Liza replied decidedly.

"That's so mean, Liza," said Chris. "He's probably shy. He didn't say much that was interesting—but not everyone can be a sparkling conversationalist, like you."

"That's true," Liza said, pretending not to know Chris was teasing. "Did you see the way he stared at Sam? He couldn't take his eyes off her."

"He did not," Sam objected, although she knew it was true.

"Get off it, you know he was," Liza said with a laugh.

The girls entered the lavish lobby with its spiral mahogany columns that stretched up to a cathedral ceiling. Decorated in gentle blues and greens, the lobby was more subdued at dinner time than it was during the busy day. Several customers lounged in the velvet chairs that were nestled together near real palms in huge brass pots.

"Hi, Mr. Schwartz," Liza called to a very old man who sat by himself, reading a paper. When there wasn't enough baby-sitting work, Liza was sometimes assigned to play checkers with the eccentric gentleman. At first he had seemed little more than a crotchety old crank, who cheated at the game every chance he could. But star-struck Liza had been fascinated to discover that Mr. Schwartz had spent many years as a Hollywood stunt man—and had worked with many old-time movie stars. Now that school had started, though, and she no longer worked in the morning, she didn't see Mr. Schwartz much.

"Where you been?" he called to her in a crackly voice.

"School started. I work afternoons now," she called back.

"Is that so," said Mr. Schwartz. "I nap afternoons. Well, I can nap later. Or earlier. Doesn't matter."

"Okay. Maybe I'll see you then," Liza said with a smile.

The girls passed through one of the hotel's three fancy restaurants. Busboys and girls in red jackets set the tables for dinner. Tuxedoed waiters stood together looking over the night's specials clipped to the leather-bound menus.

From the restaurant they walked into the stainless

21

steel kitchen, where the prep cooks who assisted Chef Alleyne were busy chopping and peeling.

Soon the girls were unchaining their bikes and riding down the long, palm-tree-lined drive away from the hotel. As Sam rode, she thought about Kyle Jameson. She knew Liza was right. He had been paying extra attention to her.

But do I like him? she asked herself. Were you supposed to feel it right away, or did the feeling grow gradually? She hadn't felt goose-bumpy or dreamy or anything that girls in books reported feeling when they felt love at first sight. But maybe that only happened in books.

Was he really boring as Liza said? Or was Chris right? Maybe he was a little shy. That was probably it. There was no denying one thing—he *was* good-looking.

And he *would* solve the no-boyfriend problem.

As if somehow reading Sam's mind, Chris turned the subject back to Kyle. "I think Sam and Kyle would make a cute couple."

"I guess," Liza mused. "They're both athletic types. But Sam would never be interested in him." Liza looked at Sam as they drove down the country road, three across on their bikes. "You're *not* interested, are you?" Liza asked.

Sam shrugged. "I don't know. Maybe I am."

Chapter Four

Sam was still thinking about boys when she propped her bike against the front porch of her house. She'd almost liked a boy once. His name was Carl. She'd met him out on her father's boat. He was one of the customers her father took out snorkeling. He'd taken her phone number, but never called.

At least it means I could like a boy if the right one came along, she told herself as she let the screen door slam behind her. *I liked Carl right away,* she remembered.

"Anybody home?" Sam called from the living room.

"We're in the kitchen," answered her sister, Greta.

Sam didn't have to guess who Greta meant by *we*. Greta was always with her surfer boyfriend, Lloyd. Greta and Lloyd were seated at the kitchen table holding hands across the red-checked cloth.

"Oh, no, the world's coming to an end!" Sam cried in mock panic. "Lloyd is in the kitchen and he's not eating!"

"Very funny, Sam," said Greta dryly.

Sam pulled open the refrigerator. "I'm shocked," she continued. "There's actually a plate of chicken left for me to eat. What's going on?"

"Nothing's going on," said Lloyd, sounding nervous. "Why do you think something's going on?" He flipped his white-blond hair out of his eyes. This was a common mannerism with Lloyd, but today he did it with more energy than usual.

"Careful, Lloyd, you're going to wrench your neck," Sam teased as she settled down at the table with the plate of cold chicken. "I was only kidding," she added.

Lloyd laughed uncomfortably. "Sure, I knew that."

Sam narrowed her eyes and studied Greta and Lloyd suspiciously. *Something is strange about them today*, she thought. Not that she didn't think they were a little strange every day.

Sam loved her sister, but they were not at all alike. Greta was into clothing, hair and the latest fads. She'd dyed her curly, naturally red hair a startling blond and always wore lots of eye makeup. Although she had just turned eighteen and was out of high school, she still seemed like a kid to Sam. Sometimes Sam felt that she was the older sister and Greta was younger.

And then there was Lloyd.

The one thing Sam could not figure out about Greta was what she saw in Lloyd. Greta might be a little spacey, but next to Lloyd she looked like Einstein. All he did all day was surf, and in the evenings he hung around the O'Neills' house. Even though he'd just turned twenty, he was showing no signs of changing this lifestyle.

It wasn't that Sam hated Lloyd. He just irritated her with his thick-headed ways. And he certainly didn't inspire Greta to any heights of achievement. As long as Lloyd was on the scene, it was enough for Greta that she was his girlfriend.

"I'd better go," said Lloyd, getting up from the table.

"*What* is going on?" Sam demanded. "You never leave before ten."

Lloyd stretched his tanned, muscular arms and yawned wide. "I had a rough day with the waves," he said.

"I'm sure. It must have been backbreaking," Sam quipped.

As usual, Lloyd didn't pick up on Sam's sarcasm, either because he chose not to, or because he didn't realize she was ribbing him. Sam was never sure which.

"Not so much the back as the upper thighs and your butt," he said. "That's where your balance comes from, really."

"Fascinating," Sam mumbled, taking another bite from her drumstick.

Greta shot Sam a look, but didn't say anything. When she spoke to Lloyd, her voice was a loving caress, soft and dreamy. "Get your rest, Lloyd," she said. "You need it."

Sam pretended to choke on her drumstick. "What does he need rest for?" she cried. "He rests all day and night."

"He does not," Greta defended him. She stood and

reached up to stroke his hair. "See you tomorrow, my love," she said.

"Man! I can't take this!" said Sam, pushing back her chair. She took the plate of chicken and continued eating it in the living room as she watched TV.

Greta and Lloyd passed her on their way out. "Later," Lloyd called to Sam, holding his hand up in a sort of unmoving wave.

"Later, Surf King," replied Sam.

In a few minutes Greta returned and peeked at the game show Sam was watching. In a moment she was hooked on the show and seated herself beside Sam on the couch.

"Chris wants to get her old hair color back," said Sam, still watching the TV. "Any chance?"

"Sure," Greta answered. "She has to dye it back to her own color so that when it comes in the roots will hardly show. Tell her to go to a hair place, though. Dyeing over dye can destroy your hair."

"I'll tell her," said Sam. She turned her attention back to the TV. The game show had ended and a different show had come on. It was called *Dateline*.

Contestants came on and told about their first date. Then the audience clapped to vote for the cutest couple.

When the commercial came on, Sam turned to Greta. "What's going on with you and Lloyd, Greta? What's all this lovey-dovey stuff about?" she asked.

Again, the dreamy, faraway look returned to Greta's eyes. "Oh, it's just that today is our anniversary. It was four years ago today that Lloyd presented me with a can of surfboard wax and asked me to be his steady."

"He gave you surfboard wax!" said Sam, rolling her green eyes.

"Well, I had told him I was planning to buy a surfboard. I thought it was sweet of him."

"You never did buy a surfboard, though," Sam reminded her.

"I know. It was a white lie. I just said it so I'd have something to talk to him about. I was always asking his advice about what kind to buy and all."

"Did you love Lloyd the minute you saw him?" Sam asked.

"The very second I saw him riding the waves, I knew he was the one," Greta said. "There was never a doubt in my mind. It was as if fate—"

"Wait a minute," Sam interrupted. "I just remembered. You used to tell me what a creep he was."

"I did?" asked Greta.

"Yes, you told me he was a big goon with the brain of an ape."

"Oh," said Greta. "I must have said that to cover up how much I really did like him. I really said that?"

"Yep."

"Well, I never thought it. I always thought Lloyd was wonderful," Greta said.

Sam got up from the couch feeling grumpy. All this love and boyfriend business was getting her down. She decided not to think about it for a while.

At that moment Sam's mother came in, carrying a

grocery bag. She had just taken their Labrador retriever, Trevor, off his leash. He bounded in alongside her.

"Hi, girls," their mother greeted them. "Everything okay?"

"Wonderful, Mother, just wonderful," Greta gushed, jumping up from the couch. "Let me help you with that bag."

Mrs. O'Neill shot Sam a quizzical glance.

"Don't ask me," Sam said with a shrug. "She's been like this since I came home."

"Where's Lloyd?" asked Mrs. O'Neill, handing Greta the bag.

"He was tired, poor dear," Greta said, following her mother into the kitchen.

"I see, another hard day at the beach," Sam heard her mother say from inside the kitchen.

Greta kept up her glowing attitude for the rest of the evening. "Is she all right?" Mr. O'Neill asked his wife over supper.

"It's her anniversary. Four years with Lloyd," Mrs. O'Neill said, by way of explaining Greta's exuberant mood.

"Where is that go-getter, Lloyd, anyway?" asked Mr. O'Neill, rubbing his dark beard. "Doesn't he usually dine with us?"

"He was tired," Greta said, her voice brimming with fondness.

"Don't tell me Lloyd got a job!" cried Mr. O'Neill.

"Nothing as mind-shattering as that, Dad," said Sam. "He just surfed too hard today."

"Oh," said Mr. O'Neill, returning to his meatloaf. "I should have realized that was an insane idea."

That evening, Greta hovered around her family, seeming unable to get enough of them. Sam tried to escape her by going upstairs to study in her bedroom, which she shared with Greta. It was no use, though. Greta followed her up. She moved restlessly around the room, obviously wanting to talk.

Sam tried to stare at her algebra book, but she couldn't concentrate. Not with Greta humming and absently rearranging things on her own cluttered dresser.

Finally giving up, Sam shut the book. "So, how's the job?" she asked Greta, referring to Greta's new office job. Greta had been a waitress at the Palm Pavilion, but now that she was out of high school, she'd decided to use the secretarial skills she'd learned in business classes. She'd just taken a job working in an auto insurance company.

"It's great!" she said, smiling. "It doesn't pay as well as waitressing, at least not at first. But I'll get raises, and I have wonderful benefits. I get health insurance, and there's a retirement plan."

"Retirement!" cried Sam. "What do you care about that?"

"I'm eighteen," Greta said knowingly. "I have to start thinking about planning a future."

Sam had never seen Greta plan anything more than two hours in advance—never mind planning for her retirement. "You're cracking up, Greta," said Sam, going back to her algebra.

Greta responded by kissing Sam on the forehead. "Well, I love you, anyway," she said.

"I love you, too," said Sam, shaking her head in bewilderment.

That night, Sam slept restlessly. At one point she dreamed that she was in the school gymnasium walking on the balance beam. When she started, there was an audience in the bleachers watching her. But when she got to the end of the beam and looked up, the bleachers were empty. A large sign on the wall read: GONE TO THE MOVIES!

Sam was roused from this dream by a sound. Groggy, she rubbed her eyes and sat up on her elbows. The sound carried her attention to the bedroom window. In the moonlight Sam saw an alarming sight.

Greta was standing outside the window on the porch roof. She was frantically yanking at her suitcase, which had become wedged in the window.

For a split second, Sam thought she was still dreaming. Then the truth hit her.

Greta was running away from home!

Chapter Five

Before Sam realized what she was doing, she was out of bed and trying to yank Greta's nylon suitcase back into the room. It was no use. The suitcase was stuck and wasn't going forward or back.

Sam craned her neck up to see over the suitcase through the upper casement of the window. She saw that Greta was all dressed up. Her hair was swept up on one side with a clip adorned with silk flowers. She had on her new pink, rose-patterned sundress, which showed off her slim waist. If it weren't for the fact that Greta was standing precariously balanced on the sloped porch roof in the middle of the night, she would have looked like any pretty girl ready for a special evening out.

"Are you crazy?" Sam cried.

Greta looked around nervously. "Shhh!"

"Where are you going?" Sam asked in an urgent whisper.

"I can't tell you," Greta replied. "Give the suitcase a push, would you?"

"No way!" Sam replied. "I'm not helping you do this."

"Sam, unless I move the suitcase, I'll be stuck out here," Greta pointed out. "Please."

Sam considered this. It was true that Greta couldn't come in with the suitcase stuck in the window. And it wouldn't come back in. Sam had already tried it.

"I'll help you if you tell me what's going on," Sam said.

"All right," Greta agreed. "After we move the suitcase. Now, you push and I'll pull."

Throwing all her weight against the bag, Sam tried to push it through the window. It budged a little, then was wedged again. "What have you got in this thing?" asked Sam. "It's so stuffed that one of the seams is ripping."

"Just keep pushing," Greta urged her.

The two sisters pushed and pulled for another five minutes, slowly working the bag through the opening. "It's almost there," said Greta. "Try giving it one hard push."

Sam put her shoulder into the side of the bag and shoved. It worked—but too well. The bag went skittering down the roof before Greta could catch it.

"Oww!" came a loud cry from below.

"Lloyd, honey!" cried Greta. Getting into a sitting position, Greta scooted her way to the end of the roof as fast as she could.

"Lloyd!" exclaimed Sam. *What is he doing down there?* Then a horrible thought struck her. "No!" she said in

32

disbelief, before the thought was even fully formed in her head. "She wouldn't."

But Sam knew it was true. Greta was eloping with Lloyd.

I have to stop her! she thought, pulling herself up into the open window. There was a bright three-quarter moon. Illuminated by its light, Sam saw Lloyd sitting on the grass below, rubbing his ankle. The suitcase was beside him. The seam had burst, probably when it had hit Lloyd, and Greta's clothes were scattered on the ground.

"Greta! Be careful!" Sam called to her sister. In her haste to reach the injured Lloyd, Greta was lowering herself from the edge of the roof.

Greta looked up at Sam. "Stay inside," she said in a hushed voice.

Sam didn't listen. *She can't make that drop*, thought Sam, coming out onto the roof. *She'll break her leg, for sure.* Sitting down as Greta had done, Sam made her way down toward her sister at the edge of the roof.

By the time she got there, Greta was already hanging from the gutter, her legs dangling almost five feet away from the porch below. Sam peeked over the edge of the roof. "Come on back up," she said, taking hold of her sister's wrist. "I'll help you."

"Stay there, Greta," said Lloyd, getting to his feet. "I'll help you down."

"She's not going down," Sam hissed at him. "She's coming up."

Greta looked at Sam with frightened eyes. "I'm afraid to go down and I can't get back up," she said.

"Don't worry, honey, I'm coming," said Lloyd as he hobbled toward Greta with his injured ankle.

"Greta, you can't go with him!" urged Sam, now holding onto both of Greta's wrists.

Suddenly Trevor began barking wildly from inside the house. The next thing Sam knew she was blinded by the porch light. When her eyes adjusted she was looking down at two angry blue eyes. "Hi, Dad," she said, letting go of Greta's wrists.

Her father held Greta's waist and lowered her down to the porch.

"Would anyone care to tell me what is going on?" he boomed, tightening the belt of his robe.

There was a long silence.

"It's like this, Mr. O'Neill," Lloyd spoke up finally.

"Yes?" inquired Mr. O'Neill, turning on him, red-faced.

"Ummm . . ." Lloyd lost his nerve in the face of Mr. O'Neill's anger.

"Lloyd and I are eloping!" Greta said boldly.

Mrs. O'Neill came out onto the porch in time to hear Greta's news. "Greta! No!" she cried, encircling Greta in her arms.

Greta pulled away from her mother. "We knew that's what you would say. That's why we were keeping it a secret," she cried.

"Darn straight that's what I would say!" shouted Mr.

34

O'Neill, incensed by the announcement. "You're eighteen, Greta!"

"Lloyd just turned twenty," Greta pouted.

"I see. Lloyd is twenty. Lloyd is twenty," Mr. O'Neill repeated, as though he couldn't believe his ears. "Does Lloyd have a job? Can Lloyd support a family?" he bellowed.

Sam had been cautiously spying from the edge of the roof. Her father's last outburst caused her to draw back. She had never—ever—seen her father so inflamed with rage. *I should probably sneak back while I can,* she thought, glancing up at her bedroom window. *Maybe he'll forget he saw me.* But she couldn't bring herself to leave. She had to know how this was going to turn out. *I won't look, I'll just sit here and listen,* she decided.

"Please, Dan," said Mrs. O'Neill. "Calm down."

"I can't calm down when Greta is about to destroy her life!"

"I'm not destroying anything, Daddy," said Greta.

"Oh, no?" replied her father. "What were you planning to live on? Love?"

"You know I have a job," Greta protested.

"Great!" Mr. O'Neill cried. "I'm overjoyed that my daughter will slave for the rest of her life to support the Surf King."

"I'm getting a job," Lloyd spoke up.

"Is that so?" said Mr. O'Neill. "And what job would that be?"

"I'm not sure yet, but I'm getting one," Lloyd told him.

Sam's curiosity got the better of her. She stretched out on her stomach and peeked over the edge of the roof. Greta was now dissolved in tears, her mascara streaming down her cheeks.

"Let's go inside and discuss this," said Mrs. O'Neill. "I'll make some coffee and we can all calm down." She opened the door, signaling them to come inside.

As if suddenly remembering his other daughter, Mr. O'Neill looked up. He locked glances with Sam.

"And what are you doing up there?" he barked. "Were you in on this, too?"

"I, uh . . . no, I . . ." Sam stammered.

He held up his arms. "Forget it, just come down from there. I don't want you falling off the roof. That's all we'd need right now." Sam sensed from his weary tone that his anger was spent. Relieved that the worst of his fury had passed, she lowered herself from the roof and dangled above the porch.

"What are you going to do?" Sam asked when he'd lowered her to the floor.

"I'm not sure," he replied. "But Lloyd is going to wish he'd never come up with this harebrained idea, I can tell you that."

Chapter Six

The next morning, Sam trudged up the steps of Bonita Beach High, yawning and bleary-eyed. She'd gone back to bed at one-thirty in the morning, leaving everyone else downstairs, still thrashing out the elopement crisis. From one-thirty until almost dawn she lay awake and listened to them argue.

As Sam approached her locker, she saw Chris leaning against it. "What happened to you?" Chris asked, shocked at Sam's bedraggled appearance.

"Do I look that bad?" Sam asked, tucking her long blond hair behind her ear.

"Worse," said Chris. "You have giant bags under your eyes—which are an attractive shade of red. Your shoulders are slumped. Even your hair looks tired."

"I meant to wash it this morning," Sam said through a yawn. "But I woke up too late."

"What's the matter?" Chris asked. "You are definitely not acting like the spritely jockette that I'm used to."

Before Sam could answer, Liza turned the corner of the hall and joined them. "Oh, my gosh!" she cried, her hand flying dramatically to her face. "What happened to you?"

Sam told them what had happened. ". . . finally, at about four-thirty in the morning, I heard Lloyd shout, 'You'll see! I'll have a job by the end of the week!' Then I heard the door slam," Sam concluded.

"I can't picture Lloyd working," Chris commented.

"Nobody can," agreed Sam.

"I would have loved to see your father's face when he came out and found Greta hanging off the porch roof," Liza said, giggling.

Sam gave a weak smile. "It must have looked pretty strange," she admitted. "But, you know, it's not really funny. It would be a catastrophe if Greta married Lloyd."

"Why?" asked Chris. "They seem to get along really well."

"I don't want my sister to marry a total flake," said Sam, taking her books from her locker and slamming it shut.

"Excuse me, but Greta isn't exactly a brain surgeon," Liza pointed out.

"She's smarter than Lloyd," Sam grumbled as they headed down the hall toward their homeroom classes. "At least she has a job."

"Speaking of Greta," said Chris. "Did you ask her about my hair?"

"Oh, yeah," said Sam. "She says go to a hair place and

have them dye it back to your natural strawberry-blond shade. Then no one will notice the slight difference as it grows in."

"Brilliant!" Chris cried gratefully. "Why didn't I think of that? I don't know how you can say Greta isn't smart, Liza. She just saved my life."

"It doesn't matter whether Greta is smart or not," said Liza. "I think she has a right to make her own decisions."

"No, she doesn't," Sam snapped. "Not if she's going to do dumb things."

Just then, a tall boy with brown curly hair came up alongside them. "Hi, cutie pie," Liza greeted her boyfriend, Eddie.

"Hi," he greeted them all. "Are we set for Saturday?" he asked Liza.

"I don't know," Liza said, glancing guiltily at Sam.

"Stop looking so guilty," Sam scolded her. "Yes, you guys are all set for Saturday," she told Eddie.

"What's the problem?" Eddie asked.

"Well, it's that the three of us were going to—" Chris began to explain.

"There is no problem," Sam cut her off.

"If you say so," said Eddie. "Look, I have to run. I have to get some homework done in homeroom. See you all later." He took off down the hallway, weaving easily between the students.

"He is adorable, isn't he?" Liza sighed as she watched him go. Then she turned to Sam with troubled eyes. "Why don't you come with us? It would really be fine."

"Look, would you please stop feeling sorry for me!" Sam snapped.

"We don't feel sorry for you," Chris objected. "We just don't want to hurt your feelings."

"I don't care. Honestly," said Sam.

"We don't mind, really we—" Liza was cut off by the sound of the buzzer telling them it was time to be inside homeroom.

"Shoot! I have to run," said Chris, whose homeroom was at the end of the hall. "Once Mr. Crabman shuts that door you're marked absent."

"If I got a boyfriend, this whole problem would be solved, wouldn't it?" Sam said to Liza as they took their seats inside their classroom.

Liza's dark eyes narrowed. "Is this a trick question?"

"Just answer me," Sam told her.

"Of course it would," Liza replied cautiously.

At that moment, Mrs. Laskin came in and began taking attendance. Sam leaned back in her chair and thought about the situation. It *wasn't* fair that Liza and Chris should be kept from doing things because of her.

The solution was pretty clear. Sam had to get a boyfriend.

Kyle Jameson's handsome face formed itself in her mind's eye. He *was* interested in her. She could tell. If she asked him out, he might say yes.

Sam had never asked a boy out. *It couldn't be that hard to do*, she figured. Girls did it all the time nowadays. Besides, maybe when she got to know Kyle better she'd like him. It was hard to tell from one conversation.

I'll do it, she decided. She owed it to Liza and Chris not to ruin their social lives. And that's exactly what she was doing by being a fifth wheel.

After homeroom, Sam told Liza her plan. "But do you even like the guy?" Liza asked.

"Maybe," replied Sam. "I have to get to know him better."

"Well, here's your chance," said Liza.

Sam followed Liza's gaze and saw Kyle coming down the hall toward them. His khaki cotton pants and crisp blue shirt were so fresh and new that he looked as if he'd stepped out of a clothing catalog.

Suddenly aware of her limp hair, Sam shoved both sides behind her ears. She wished she'd taken a little more time to primp this morning.

"Hi," she said when he spotted Liza and Sam. Again, his blue eyes were fixed on Sam.

"Hi—bye, I have to run," Liza excused herself diplomatically. She hurried off down the hall, leaving Sam alone with Kyle.

I can't do it, thought Sam. *I can't ask him out. I don't even know him*. She had to, though. It was the only solution.

"How's it going?" asked Kyle.

"Okay," Sam replied awkwardly. "How do you like working at the Palm so far?"

Kyle smiled. Sam noticed that he had nice, straight white teeth. "You were right about that guy Parker. He notices everything," said Kyle.

41

"He can drive you crazy," Sam said with a laugh. "But he's not as bad as he seems. Not quite as bad, anyway."

They continued talking about the Palm Pavilion. Sam stayed on the topic, glad to be able to fill Kyle in on the workings of the hotel and little bits of harmless gossip she knew about the different employees. It was a safe topic, one she felt comfortable with.

Kyle folded his arms and leaned against the wall. He seemed interested in everything she said. He laughed at the funny stories she told about the run-ins she, Liza and Chris had had with Mr. Parker over the summer.

He laughed especially hard when she recounted how she and Liza had gotten stuck hiding in a famous actor's shower while Mr. Parker was in the other room checking the air conditioning. "We just wanted to see a real star's room. I thought we'd never get out of there," gasped Sam, breathless with laughter.

"What did you do?" asked Kyle, smiling.

"Oh, we managed to bolt for the door when Parker wasn't looking," she said, holding her sides.

At that moment the first bell of the morning rang. "I know we just met," Kyle began quickly. "But I already feel like I know you. I was wondering if you'd like to do something with me this weekend."

All right! thought Sam jubilantly. "What did you have in mind?" she asked.

"I don't know. The movies . . . maybe dinner," he suggested.

"Okay, sure," she agreed, trying not to look too happy and eager.

"Great," he said. "I guess we'd better get to class. I'll call you later."

"Bye," said Sam as he hurried off down the hall. *Boy,* she thought happily. *For a day that started off so badly, things are definitely looking up.*

Chapter Seven

That same Tuesday, after school, Sam worked at the Palm Pavilion with Chris and Liza. This time, Courtney Rutherford was assigned to her.

Sam met Courtney's mother in the lobby. She was a tall, elegant woman with sleek blond hair pulled back into a French twist. "I asked Mr. Parker to assign you to Courtney," Mrs. Rutherford told Sam. "Courtney adores you, and, frankly speaking, some baby sitters don't have much luck with her. She's such a headstrong child, not everyone can control her."

"She's a good kid," said Sam. "But I know what you mean."

Courtney smiled at Sam. "Can we play sea horsie again today?"

"Sure," said Sam, taking Courtney's small hand.

The afternoon passed quickly. Sam had figured out that the key to keeping Courtney happy was to keep her busy. So, while Chris paddled around the pool with

Esmee, Sam kept Courtney moving. They ran races up and down the beach behind the pools. They collected shells, dug holes, played catch and made believe they were Snow White and the Seven Dwarfs.

Courtney decided that she would be Snow White and Sam would play the roles of all seven dwarfs.

"I have never been so tired in my whole life," said Sam as the girls rode home from work together at five-thirty. "Even Courtney noticed. She said that of all my dwarf impressions, I did Sleepy the best."

Liza chuckled. "If I had to take care of that kid again, I would have been acting like Grumpy."

"I can't imagine minding her if I only had three hours' sleep, like you did," added Chris.

They were riding their bicycles through downtown Bonita Beach, which was really just a cluster of small shopping arcades, a few restaurants and bars, a movie theater and a bunch of government buildings on either side of a two-lane highway. They rode three across, only going to single file to avoid cars, which passed about every ten minutes.

"It wasn't too bad in the beginning of my shift," said Sam. "I was so excited about my date with Kyle that it gave me a second wind." She'd told Chris and Liza about Kyle right after school.

"Do you really like him?" Liza questioned skeptically.

"That's what I'll find out," Sam answered. "Isn't that why you go on a date? To find out if you like each other?"

"It's amazing," said Chris. "On Monday you were

45

worried about not having a boyfriend. And just one day later, you have one."

"He's not my boyfriend. Not yet," said Sam.

"The guy's crazy about you, though," Chris observed. "It was like love at first sight for him."

They turned off the highway and up Vine Street, a residential street of small wood and stucco houses. Their first stop was Chris's neat yellow house. Sam and Liza said good-bye to her and rode on together until they came to the corner where they usually went their separate ways.

"What is it you don't like about Kyle?" Sam asked Liza as they came to a stop at the corner.

"I'm not sure." Liza shrugged.

"If things work out between us, then you won't have to worry about my feelings when you and Chris go out," Sam pointed out, in case Liza had missed the obvious advantage of Sam's dating Kyle.

"That would solve the problem," Liza admitted. She checked her purple plastic watch. "Wow! It's quarter to six. I have to get home. My mother's working a night shift at the hospital and I have to take care of the twins."

Sam rubbed her eyes wearily. "If I had to do one more thing tonight I'd cry."

Liza started to take off on her bike, then put her feet down again after two turns of the pedal. "Hey," she called back to Sam. "I meant to tell you. I saw a sign at school saying there's going to be a gymnastics practice tomorrow afternoon."

"I know," Sam called back. "The big tryouts are on Thursday."

"Get some sleep, huh?" shouted Liza.

"Okay!" said Sam. *If I can keep Greta off the roof, I will*, she added to herself. She rode on to a large white house and turned up the dirt drive beside it. Her house was the smaller one behind it. The big house belonged to people who only came down in the winter, usually by November.

Sam noticed Greta's beat-up blue Mustang in the driveway. It stood behind the van her father used to pick up and drop off customers for his snorkeling tours. Sam stopped and looked at the big, loopy, hot-pink writing on the side of the van. *Captain Dan's Snorkeling Tours*, it read.

Greta had done the writing during the time when she was learning calligraphy. As far as Sam was concerned, it just looked like sloppy script. She couldn't believe that her father had actually allowed Greta to write on his van. Her penmanship was terrible. But, that was Greta—always plunging right in, whether she was ready or not.

And Mr. O'Neill didn't seem to mind. If something made Greta or Sam happy, that was what mattered. He was an easygoing father, indulging both his daughters when he could. He was quick to overlook small infractions of the rules, as long as no one was hurt.

That's why Sam hadn't been prepared for the ferocity of his anger last night. The only other time she'd ever seen him so infuriated was once when she was in the fourth grade. An older boy had punched Sam in the eye

47

on the way home from school. She showed up crying on the front porch, her eye already on its way to purple. While her mother called the doctor, Sam saw her father's face turn crimson with rage. "Nobody hurts my little girl," he had growled as he flew out of the house to see the boy's parents.

As soon as Sam got into the house she saw that nothing had been resolved. Her father had obviously just come in from work. He was wearing his usual Captain Dan outfit: a tropical shirt, pants and his navy-and-white captain's hat. He stood stubbornly in the middle of the room, his arms folded.

"You are so unfair!" Greta whimpered. She looked even more exhausted than Sam. Dark bags sat under her red-rimmed eyes. She had just come home from work, too. She was dressed in a blue suit she'd just bought in order to look "corporate."

"I've been thinking about it all day," Mr. O'Neill said. "And that's my rule. I don't want to see Lloyd here until he has a job."

"You can't stop me from seeing Lloyd," Greta said firmly.

"Maybe not. But I don't have to feed the deadbeat."

Greta burst into tears. "You're being so horrible," she cried through her tears.

Poor Greta, thought Sam. She hated seeing her so upset.

At that moment, her father noticed her standing there. "Thank goodness *you're* not dating," he said. "At least I have one sensible daughter."

"Thanks a lot, Daddy!" Greta cracked through her tears.

"Well, Sam knows that her teen years should be spent doing things, learning, not wasting her time dating some nitwit."

Sam didn't like the position her father was putting her in. She didn't want to be used to make Greta feel bad. "Actually," Sam spoke up, wanting to give Greta some support, "I do have a date. He's a new—"

"Oh, no you don't!" bellowed Mr. O'Neill.

"Why not?" Sam asked indignantly.

"You're not dating until you're sixteen. And then I'll *think* about it!" her father informed her.

"You let Greta date when she was fourteen!" cried Sam.

"And look what happened!" shouted Mr. O'Neill, pointing at Greta. "She thinks a boob like Lloyd is a catch. She should never have dated so young. It stunted her development."

"That is *it*!" shrieked Greta. "I am *not* a case of stunted development!" Greta stomped out of the living room and went up the stairs, closing the door to her bedroom with a resounding slam.

Mr. O'Neill stood there, rubbing his dark beard. Sam turned and saw her mother hurrying in the front door. "What's going on now?" she asked.

"Mom!" Sam said to her mother. "Dad says I can't date."

"You have a date?" her mother asked.

"Yeah, and he's a cute guy, but now Dad says I can't,"

she spoke in an anxious rush. This couldn't be happening. She finally got a date and she couldn't go! "Mom, I can go, can't I?"

Mrs. O'Neill took a deep breath. "Dan, maybe you should think about—"

"I've thought about nothing else all day, Maureen," he said to his wife. "In a way, this is all our fault. We were wrong to let Greta date so young. She got so caught up with Lloyd she never developed herself. We're not making the same mistake with Sam."

"That's not fair, Dad," said Sam. "I'm not Greta. I'm totally dif—"

"I said no!" Mr. O'Neill exploded. "And that's final!"

Chapter Eight

Kyle Jameson was leaning against Sam's locker when she got to school the next morning. Once again, he looked neat and pressed, as if he were a clothing ad somehow come to life.

"Hi," he said, straightening up.

"Hi," she answered, trying to look lighthearted and carefree. That wasn't how she felt, though. The tense atmosphere in her home had put her in a bad mood. And, more important right now, she hadn't figured out a way to tell Kyle she couldn't date him.

"Have you thought of anything you'd like to do this Saturday?" Kyle asked.

"No, ummm, anything would be okay," she said.

As Sam pulled books from her locker, not even bothering to see if they were the ones she needed, Liza and Chris came down the hall.

"Hi," said Liza, stopping at Sam's locker. "Sam told me you guys are going out Saturday."

"That's right," said Kyle.

"We're going to the movies Saturday," Liza told him. "Chris is going with Bruce, who you might know because he works at the Palm. And I'm going with Eddie. He goes to school here, too."

"They're not seniors, are they?" Kyle asked.

"No, Bruce is a sophomore and Eddie is a junior," Chris told him. "Why don't you two come with us? It'll be fun."

Oh, no! thought Sam. She hadn't had a chance to tell Chris or Liza about her father's new rule.

"I don't think we can," Kyle cut in abruptly. "I made plans already."

Plans? thought Sam, confused. *He didn't have any a minute ago.*

"Okay, maybe another time," said Liza.

The first bell of the day sounded. "Are you coming?" Liza asked Sam.

"I want to talk to Sam for a second," said Kyle.

"All right," said Liza, sounding slightly miffed. "See you in homeroom."

"What plans have you got?" Sam asked Kyle when Chris and Liza were gone.

"I just said that to get out of going with them," he answered.

"Why?" Sam asked.

"I don't want to go out with them. I want to go out with you," he said as they started walking down the hall. "You seem so different from Chris and Liza," he added after a moment.

"Different?" Sam asked. "How?"

Kyle stopped walking and smiled at her. "The minute I saw you, I could tell. You're not giddy and silly like other girls your age."

Sam had always been called sensible, so Kyle's words rang true to her.

"There's something very special about you, Samantha." He stopped, as if listening to the echo of his own words. "I think I'm going to call you Samantha from now on."

Sam wrinkled her nose in displeasure. "Nobody else does. I'm not used to it. It's not exactly my favorite name."

"It's a great name," he disagreed. "Sam is a boy's name. Samantha is all female, and you are definitely a female."

A hot blush swept across Sam's forehead. Of course she was female! But he made it sound like a strange, alien thing to be. Still, although they made her uncomfortable, his words were sort of thrilling. It was enticing to think of herself as older, more mature than her classmates. A female, not a girl.

"I guess you can call me Samantha if you like," she said.

For the rest of the morning, Sam's mind was not on her schoolwork. There were so many other things to think about. She *had* to go out on this date with Kyle! There had to be a way to convince her father to change his mind.

She was also busy thinking about the gymnastics

practice that afternoon. Her gym teacher, Mrs. Pruett, had told them a little about it in class. Gymnastics team members would be expected to concentrate on only one piece of equipment. Sam couldn't decide between the balance beam or the uneven parallel bars. She was good at both of them, but stronger on the beam.

At lunchtime, Kyle was once again at her locker. "Want to have lunch together?" he asked.

"I'd like to," Sam said, "but I always eat with Liza and Chris."

"Would they mind if you skipped it this once?" he asked.

"I guess not," Sam agreed.

When Sam and Kyle reached the cafeteria, Liza and Chris were already there, talking to Bruce and Eddie. "Come on," Sam said. "I'll introduce you."

Looking reluctant, Kyle followed Sam over to the group. "Eddie, this is Kyle," Sam introduced him. "And this is Bruce," she said, nodding at the blond, broad-shouldered boy Chris was crazy about.

"Kyle just started working at the Palm," Chris told the boys.

"Great, we'll probably work together sometime," said Bruce as he shook hands with Kyle. "Hey, Sam," he added. "What's with Lloyd?" Bruce and Eddie were also surfers—and they admired Lloyd for his skill with a surfboard and what they called his "total coolness."

"Lloyd didn't surf yesterday. We went down to Castaway Beach after school, and no Lloyd," added Eddie, also shaking Kyle's hand.

"Sorry for talking about this guy you don't know," Bruce apologized to Kyle. "It's just that we're worried about him. He didn't surf yesterday and someone told us they saw him looking really down and going into all the stores over at the mall."

"He must be looking for a job," Sam guessed. She told them what had happened. ". . . And my father won't let him in the house unless he has a job," she finished.

"You mean we might lose The Surf Master?" cried Eddie. "We depend on him to be there. He's like a symbol of surfing. Something constant that you can depend on in a changing world."

"Don't you think Greta should be able to depend on him if they want to get married?" said Sam.

"She can depend on him to surf," said Bruce.

"You guys!" Liza laughed. "You'd think surfing was the only thing in the world."

Bruce and Eddie pretended to be offended. "We know there's more to life than surfing," said Bruce.

"Sure," added Eddie. "There's snorkeling and water-skiing."

Everyone laughed. Except Kyle. He only smiled politely. Sam wondered if he thought they were juvenile and silly. After all, even she had thought that about most surfers—though not Eddie and Bruce, of course. They were great.

"Kyle and I were going to have lunch together," Sam said, looking from Liza to Chris. "You don't mind, do you?"

"Sure, don't worry about it," Liza told her.

Sam and Kyle got their food and sat down to lunch. She shuffled in her chair, feeling uncomfortable as Kyle stared at her. "I remembered another funny story about Mr. Parker," Sam began, trying to recapture the ease of yesterday's conversation. She started to tell him about the time a parrot had escaped from the Parrot Lounge at the Palm Pavilion. But she couldn't concentrate on the story. She was distracted by Kyle's unswerving gaze. "I wish you wouldn't keep staring at me," she said, finally.

"I can't help it," he said. "You're just so pretty."

Sam looked down at her tray of food. "Thank you," she replied. No boy had ever said anything like that to her before. This was all so confusing. She didn't know how she felt.

The business of having a boyfriend was turning out to be more complicated than she'd thought.

Chapter Nine

"So, today's the big day," Liza said to Sam as they left homeroom together the next day, Thursday.

"What do you mean?" asked Sam.

"Gymnastics tryouts!" cried Liza. "Which piece did you decide to try out on?" Liza asked as they joined the throng of students changing classes.

"I don't know yet," Sam admitted.

"Which piece did you practice on yesterday?"

Sam pretended to fiddle with the setting of her watch. "I didn't go to the practice," she said, trying to sound unconcerned.

"You didn't *what*?" yelled Liza.

"I didn't go. Kyle met me on my way to the gym and he wanted to go for pizza. I said I couldn't, but he got all bent out of shape. He acted like I was trying to avoid him," Sam explained.

"So what?" Liza said.

"So, I didn't want him to think that," Sam spoke

defensively. "My father has decided that I'm not allowed to date until I'm sixteen, so I want to spend as much time with Kyle as I can before I tell him the bad news. I have to make sure he knows I like him before I say I can't go."

"Sixteen!" Liza gasped. "That's two whole years away! How come?"

"Greta," Sam replied simply. "Because of her, Dad thinks I'm going to try to elope with the first boy I date."

"He'll change his mind," Liza said encouragingly.

"I don't know," said Sam. "I asked again last night and he said his mind was made up."

"That's terrible," Liza sympathized. "And totally unfair."

"No kidding," grumbled Sam.

They walked along down the hall without speaking. "But getting back to gymnastics . . ." Liza said after a few moments. "What are you going to do?"

"There's another practice today at lunchtime," Sam said.

Liza sighed skeptically. "Good luck. I hope one practice is enough."

Sam left Liza and went on to her first-period math class. The class seemed to go on forever. So did the entire morning. Sam was dying to get to that lunchtime practice. *It will all come back to me once I'm there,* she thought hopefully. Still, she hadn't done any gymnastics since last November when they'd covered it in gym. That was almost a year ago.

When the lunch bell finally sounded, she raced to her

locker for her sneakers and shorts. She was almost around the corner when she stopped short.

Kyle was waiting by her locker.

She ducked back behind the corner. If he saw her he'd want to eat lunch with her again. And if she tried to tell him she couldn't, he might act insulted, or talk her out of going to practice.

As she stood, hovering near the wall, she saw Chris come down the hall. "Chris," she called urgently, waving her friend over. "I need your help."

"What's the matter?" Chris asked, her eyes wide with concern.

"You have to go to my locker and get my gym stuff."

"Is there any particular reason why *I* have to do this?" Chris asked suspiciously.

Sam pointed around the corner to her locker. Chris took a quick peek and then jerked her head back. "I thought you liked Kyle?" she said.

"I do," Sam spoke anxiously. "But if he sees me, he'll want to have lunch with me. If I say no, then he'll think I don't like him, but I have to go to this lunchtime practice. And—"

"Whoa!" Chris stopped her. "I get the picture. I've never seen you like this. Are you okay?"

"Fine. Are you going to help me out or not?" Sam demanded.

"Okay, okay. Liza told me about your father's 'no dating' rule. What a drag!"

"I know, but I can't talk now. Please go get my stuff."

Chris nodded. "All right. I think I remember your

combination. Six to the left, two to the right, four left?"

"Right. I mean correct, four to the left," Sam confirmed.

Sam pressed her spine into the cool tile wall and waited while Chris went to her locker. In a few moments, Chris returned with the running shorts, T-shirt and sneakers Sam used for gym. "He asked if I knew where you were, and I said I didn't know," Chris told her. "I said I was borrowing this stuff."

"Thanks, Chris. You're a pal," said Sam. With her books and gym things in her arms, she raced through the halls down to the gym. She quickly changed and entered the gym.

The gymnasium was crowded with girls gathered around the various pieces. In one corner were the uneven parallel bars. In another stood the horse. The balance beam was in the middle of the room. Juniors and seniors wearing leotards worked out on each piece, demonstrating different moves to the younger girls.

Sam stood and considered which piece to go to.

"The beam," she said to herself impulsively. Last year, her gym teacher, Mrs. Kline, had told her she had terrific natural balance. And Sam had enjoyed learning the beam more than she had the other pieces. That was the one she'd try for.

She joined the crowd watching the balance beam demonstration. A senior named Karen moved across the smooth wood with the poise of a ballerina. She demonstrated a forward roll, a high kick and a split.

I can do that, thought Sam.

But when Sam's chance came to go through a routine, she found that she was shaky. She slipped off the beam as she tried to do a backward roll. "I don't understand. I could do it last year," she told Karen.

"It's easy to forget," said Karen. "That's why we're having these practices. The judges will want to see a mount, a roll and one other move."

Sam saw other freshmen practicing on the floor nearby. She joined them, finding a line in the floor to use as her pretend beam. She watched the other girls carefully. It was clear that they'd attended the earlier practice. They seemed to know lots of moves that she'd never seen before.

After the practice, Sam grabbed a sandwich at the cafeteria and ran to class. She spent the day hardly hearing her teachers. She was going through the balance beam moves in her mind's eye. The backward roll worried her the most. She hadn't gotten a chance to try it again.

At the last bell, Sam didn't bother to go to her locker. She'd kept her gym things with her all afternoon. She told herself it was so she could get down to the gym as quickly as possible. She didn't want to admit to herself that she was also ducking Kyle once again.

The tryouts were even more crowded than the practice had been. She gave her name to Mrs. Pruett, who was judging the balance beam tryouts.

When Sam's turn came she hopped up on the beam, using the springboard. She wobbled at first, but didn't fall off. *Steady, steady,* she urged herself. After a few

61

steps she managed a high kick. And then a second and a third.

"Nice," she heard Mrs. Pruett whisper off to the side.

Next came the backward roll. Lying flat on the beam, Sam grasped the smooth wood surface behind her. She hung her head to the side and, using her stomach muscles for control, she pulled her legs over her head. *Slowly*, she coached herself.

The next thing she knew, she was on the floor. *Swell*, she thought, disgusted with her performance. *Great job, Sam.*

"Not bad," said Mrs. Pruett as Sam walked past her.

Sam smiled thinly at the young gym teacher. Surely she was just being nice. In the locker room, she slumped down onto the bench. How had she managed to mess up something so important to her? Why had she thought having pizza with Kyle was more important than making that practice?

Chapter Ten

After gymnastics tryouts, Sam had to hurry to the Palm. She'd told Mr. Parker she was going to be an hour late. But as she chained her bike to the rack at the side of the hotel, she checked her watch and saw that she was an hour and fifteen minutes late.

Sam ran up the side walkway and into the service entrance. She grabbed her timecard and punched it into the clock. The timecard was a precise record of when she came in and when she left. There was no way to get around it. "Shoot!" she muttered as she read the time inscription. Three-forty-seven. She'd been hoping that her watch was fast.

"Shoot, indeed," came a familiar voice.

Sam looked up from her card and found herself facing Mr. Parker. "Sorry, Mr. Parker," she began. "I had tryouts for the gymnastics team and they ran later than I expected. I—"

"You are late, Miss O'Neill," said Mr. Parker, ignoring

her excuse. He took her timecard from her hand and read it. "You are seventeen minutes later than the already late hour that we agreed upon."

"It won't happen again," said Sam.

"No, it won't," said Mr. Parker. "It was with grave misgivings that I allowed you girls to stay on after the summer. I do not wish to be blamed for any academic falling off, nor do I wish to inhibit you in the carefree enjoyment of your youth. Nonetheless, since you girls were so zealous in your pleas for continued employment, I relented."

"We appreciate that, sir," said Sam anxiously. "You don't know how much." She was becoming scared that her lateness might get all of them fired.

"Be that as it may," Mr. Parker continued, "I have a hotel to run. I am not a social director, a nursemaid or a guidance counselor. If you find you do not have the time to fit us into your jam-packed schedule, then please—"

"Oh, I do have time to fit you in . . . I mean, I want to fit you in . . . no, no, it's no problem fitting this in. I love working here, really," Sam spoke hurriedly.

"Very well then," said Mr. Parker. "Miss Velez and Miss Brown have taken on little Miss Rutherford, but I'm sure they anxiously await your overdue arrival. You will find them out by the pool."

"Thank you, Mr. Parker," said Sam, backing away from the hotel manager. When he had gone off to consult with Chef Alleyne about the night's menu, Sam ran through the kitchen, into one of the restaurants and out through the lobby.

She had just run through the sliding glass doors that led out to the pools when she almost bumped into Kyle. "Samantha, where have you been all day? I've been—"

"I can't talk to you now, Kyle," she said as she looked down to the far pool for Chris and Liza. She spotted them playing with the kids in the water. "I'd like to, but I'm so late."

Kyle took her hand. "Come on, you've got one minute for me. I haven't seen you all day."

"Okay, a minute," Sam reluctantly agreed.

"Where were you today?" he asked.

"I'm sorry, Kyle. I had gymnastics tryouts today."

"All day?" he said, sounding hurt.

"No, no, of course not," she replied. As she spoke, she felt the sensation of someone looking at her. It was Mr. Parker. He stood in the lobby and was staring at her through the glass doors. "Look, Kyle, I can't talk now," she said, panicked. "I have to go, that's all."

Not waiting for his reply, Sam rushed to the far pool.

"How did it go?" asked Liza as Sam approached.

"Don't ask," said Sam. "I am having a totally horrible day." She undressed down to the bathing suit she wore under her clothing. Then she got into the water with Chris and Liza. "How is Courtney doing?" she inquired.

Courtney was floating a boat by herself over in the corner of the pool. "Well, she had a fight with Yvonne and Judy over there," said Chris, pointing out two new little girls who were swimming together off to the other side. "She's calm now, though. She's pretending she's the pirate queen or something."

"Should we leave her there all by herself?" asked Sam, concerned.

"Forget it," said Liza. "We offered to play with her. She's in her own little fantasy world. She doesn't want to be bothered."

"Good." Sam sighed. "I couldn't deal with her right now."

"Why was your day so terrible?" asked Chris.

"I bombed out on the gymnastics tryouts. Then I got in trouble with Parker for being late. I practically had to run away from Kyle just now because Parker saw me talking to him." Sam squinted into the sun, trying to find Kyle. He was busy hosing down the pool area closest to the hotel.

At that moment the rubber band that held Sam's hair back in a ponytail snapped. "I don't believe this!" cried Sam. "Everything is coming apart!" She sat down on the side of the pool and covered her eyes with her hand. She wanted the world to go away, just for one minute.

"It's only a rubber band, Sam," said Liza. "I have another one."

"It's not the rubber band," Sam said. "It's everything. Everyone in my house is either mad or tense or sad. Parker just yelled at me. I can forget about being on the gymnastics team. I can't deal with all this and have a boyfriend, too."

"A boyfriend is supposed to make you happy," Liza pointed out.

"I *am* happy that Kyle likes me," said Sam. "He just seems to take up a lot of time."

"Maybe you guys haven't adjusted to each other yet," said Chris. "It's only been a few days."

"I guess," said Sam. "Right now, I just want to go home and hide under the covers."

Just then, Courtney spotted Sam. "Come see my pirate ship," she called to her.

"Boy, *we* weren't allowed near the pirate ship," said Liza, pretending to be insulted.

"She probably wants me to walk the plank," Sam joked ruefully.

The girls spent the next hour playing with the kids. Yvonne and Judy forgot their feud with Courtney when she promised to let them have some of her pirate treasure. This led to a game of digging for treasure down on the beach. Sam, Chris and Liza secretly wrapped fifty cents up in a tissue and stuck it inside someone's abandoned sand castle.

"I told you there was treasure," said Courtney, seeming completely unsurprised when they uncovered the money.

Throwing herself into the game improved Sam's spirits a little. As she walked back to the hotel lobby with Chris, Liza and the kids, she kept her eye out for Kyle. She wanted to talk to him, have him tell her how pretty she was. That would make her feel much better.

She didn't see him, though. At the time clock, she pulled out his card. "Gee, he left five minutes ago," she said, reading the time imprint. "You'd think he would have waited for me."

Chapter Eleven

The next morning, at school, Sam noticed a crowd of girls gathered near the gym bulletin board. *They're checking to see who made gymnastics*, she realized. She wanted to run over and see if her name was on the list, but a big lump formed in her throat and she felt like she was planted in quicksand.

Suddenly a girl from her homeroom named Helen called out her name and startled her. "Congratulations!"

Sam checked over her shoulder to see if Helen was speaking to someone else. "You're alternate on the beam," Helen said, smiling.

"What?" asked Sam.

"You're the permanent substitute," came a voice from behind Sam. It was Mrs. Pruett, the gym teacher. "You're a natural, Sam."

"Gee, you really think so? I mean, except for the practices, I haven't done gymnastics since last year's gym class."

"Well, I can see you certainly have ability, so I put you on as an alternate. You'll fill in at meets if one of the regular four girls can't make it, or is injured. If you work hard and really improve, I'll put you on the team as a regular."

"I'll improve," Sam assured Mrs. Pruett happily. "You can count on that."

Mrs. Pruett laughed lightly. "Well, you already have the spirit I like to see."

"You won't be sorry," Sam told her. "Thanks for the chance."

Sam headed for her locker, elated. Although this was the first time in her life that she hadn't made a team she'd tried for, she *had* squeaked through. She was sure that once she practiced the balance beam she'd be as good as—no, better than—the others.

It would mean work, though. Serious work.

I can't let Kyle distract me, either, she resolved. *If I had gone to that first practice, I'd probably be on the team right now.*

As Sam neared her locker, she was surprised that no one was there waiting for her. She stayed there a few minutes, straightening her books. No one came by—not even Liza or Chris. *I guess they figured Kyle would be here,* Sam realized.

This realization made her sad. She'd wanted a boy-friend so she could do dating things with Chris and Liza. But it was having the opposite effect. She was seeing them less than ever. The other day she hadn't eaten lunch with them. Now they weren't even at her locker.

Was this the price they were going to have to pay for having boyfriends? Losing their friendship? No. Sam didn't want to believe it. There had to be a way to balance both things.

The first bell of the day went off and Sam headed for homeroom. Liza was already seated when Sam arrived. "Hey, way to go," Liza said to Sam. "I checked the bulletin board on my way in."

"I'm only a sub," said Sam, taking her seat across from Liza. "But Mrs. Pruett says if I improve I can be on the team, so I'm definitely going to work at it."

"Boy, you're going to be busy," Liza said. "You'll have school, the Palm Pavilion and gymnastics—not to mention Kyle."

"I'll have to make Kyle understand, that's all." Sam spoke confidently, but she was worried. Would he understand? She wasn't sure.

That morning, as Sam changed classes, she kept a lookout for Kyle. She spotted him walking down the hall with a group of seniors after third period. Sam called to him but he didn't seem to hear. He disappeared into a classroom before she could reach him.

Oh, well, she told herself, *I'll see him at lunch.* But when lunchtime came, Kyle didn't come to her locker. Sam couldn't find him in the cafeteria, either. "Where could he be?" she muttered, crossing the cafeteria. "Doesn't he even want to hear how tryouts went?"

Sam spotted Liza and Chris at the far end of the cafeteria. "What do you think?" asked Chris, touching her hair. She'd dyed it strawberry blond, a shade brighter than her own natural color.

"It looks good," Sam said absently. She was still checking the cafeteria for Kyle.

"Where's Kyle?" asked Chris, sensing Sam's concern.

"What do you mean, where's Kyle?" asked Sam, annoyed. "Am I supposed to be with him every minute?"

"Excuse me," Chris replied. "You have been eating lunch with him, haven't you?"

"Sorry," Sam apologized. "I don't know where he is." Sam noticed that Liza and Chris had bought wrapped sandwiches instead of food on a tray.

"We're going to sit outside and eat with Bruce and Eddie," Chris explained.

"We figured you'd be eating with Kyle," added Liza. "But since you're not, do you want to eat with us?"

"No, thanks," said Sam, not wanting to feel like a tagalong. "I'll wait for Kyle. I'm sure he'll be here soon."

When Chris and Liza were gone, Sam bought a hamburger and found a seat by herself. She knew most of the kids, but she felt awkward inviting herself to join them for lunch since she'd never done so before.

It felt strange to be eating alone. She was suddenly conscious of chewing. Her burger seemed to take forever to chew. And she didn't know where to rest her eyes. She didn't want to make eye contact with everyone who passed, as though she were longing for a friend. But it seemed odd to simply stare down at her food as though she found it fascinating. Sam wished she hadn't left her books in her locker. At least then she could have pretended to be studying.

Sam wolfed down her lunch and left the cafeteria. Lunchtime usually seemed too brief. Today it took an eternity as Sam organized the bottom half of her locker, not knowing what else to do with the time. *If this keeps up I'll have to start a locker organizing service*, she said to herself with a baleful laugh.

During the afternoon, Sam concentrated on what was being said in class. She'd been so distracted all week that she needed to catch up with what was going on.

At the end of her last class, Sam took the long way around to her locker—the way that would bring her past Kyle's locker. She walked past slowly, pretending to be reading over an old test paper. Out of the corner of her eye, she checked Kyle's locker. It was shut tight, and he wasn't there. *He's gone home*, she thought. *He left without even speaking to me!*

At that moment, panic set in. Maybe Kyle was angry with her. She should have been nicer to him, not ducked him during school yesterday. And then, she'd run away from him at the Palm. He was probably furious with her.

As she rounded the corner to her locker, her heart skipped a beat. There stood Kyle, looking as neat and carefully put together as ever. "There you are!" Sam cried. "Where have you been?"

"I've been around," he said coolly.

Sam saw his point instantly. He was giving her back a taste of her own medicine.

"I'm sorry about yesterday. I told you I had gymnastics practice and then tryouts," she said. "And then I just couldn't talk to you. Parker was watching me."

He listened but didn't reply. She could tell from his expression that he *was* angry. "I have some good news, though," Sam rambled on nervously. "I made the team. Well, almost. I'm an alternate."

Kyle barely seemed to hear her good news. "That's nice," he said. "I don't see why you couldn't have told me you were going to practice and tryouts yesterday."

"I couldn't, Kyle," said Sam. "I was afraid you'd want me to go somewhere with you. I was afraid you'd talk me out of going."

Kyle's brow knit into a frown. "Maybe I would have," he admitted. "I want a girlfriend who has time for me. I don't need someone who squeezes me in between activities."

Sam didn't know how to reply. She was too busy trying to absorb all he'd just said. The word "girlfriend" kept running through her mind. It sounded so good. It would be wonderful to be someone's girlfriend. . . .

But what about everything else he'd said? He wanted someone with lots of time to devote to him. Time was one thing she wouldn't have if she wanted to be on the team and keep her job at the Palm.

She couldn't think about all that now. She had to concentrate on keeping him from breaking off with her.

"I'm only an alternate," she told him. "I'll have more time than if I'd actually made the team."

He smiled at this. "That's good," he said. He draped

one arm across her shoulder. "Because I hope you're as serious about us as I am."

I've hardly known you for a full week, thought Sam. Could a serious relationship develop in a week? She certainly didn't think of them as *us*.

"I am serious," she answered, afraid to express her real thoughts.

Kyle leaned in and brushed her lips lightly with a kiss. Sam's eyes darted around to see if anyone was watching. She wasn't comfortable with the idea of kissing in the hallway.

He tried to kiss her again. This time she backed away. "Kyle, come on, don't," she said in a small voice.

"What's the matter?" he asked, sounding hurt. "You don't want me to kiss you?"

"It's not that," Sam replied. "There are people around."

"So?" he asked. "Don't you want them to see us together?"

"It's not that. It's just embarrassing." There was something else that Sam didn't want to tell him. She'd never been kissed by a boy before. She'd imagined it, dreamed about it even. She didn't want her first kiss to be in a public school hallway. That didn't fit the romantic picture in her mind one bit.

"You know what you're acting like?" he said. "A freshman. Maybe I was wrong about you being more mature than the others. You're not any different."

"Yes, I am," Sam heard herself say. "Kissing in public makes me uncomfortable, that's all."

"Well, maybe a little more kissing will help you get over that," he teased, kissing her one more time.

When he was done, he rested against her locker. "I have something to ask you," he said. "My parents are giving a party tonight, and they want me to show. I'd like you to come. That will be a good way for you to meet Mom and Dad, too."

"Tonight!" Sam gasped.

"I was going to ask you yesterday, but I didn't get a chance to talk to you, remember?"

"You should have called me up."

Kyle shrugged. "I was a little mad at you by last night. Now I'm not anymore. So what do you say?"

A sickening feeling began to grow in Sam's stomach. Her father would definitely consider this a date! She couldn't tell Kyle she was forbidden to date now—not after he'd just implied that maybe she was too young for him. He'd dump her in a second if he found out she couldn't date.

Then where would she be? Out in the cold, without a boyfriend once again. There had to be a way to go to this party!

"Sure, I'd love to go," she said. "I have to work this afternoon, though. What time is it?"

"Eight. If you give me directions, I can pick you up."

"Ummm," Sam stalled. There was no way he could come to her house. She needed some time to think of what to do. "I, uh, I'll call you. The directions are kind of complicated. I'll call you as soon as I get out of work today. Promise."

"Great," he replied, putting his arm around her.

Sam discovered that she enjoyed walking down the hall with a handsome boy's arm around her. It made her feel important.

I'm going on this date, no matter what, she decided then and there.

Chapter Twelve

"I'm just going to walk out the door," Sam said boldly, later that afternoon. "There's nothing my father will be able to do to stop me."

"Want to bet?" quipped Liza. The girls had gotten permission to take the kids they were sitting for down to the Palm's luxurious, palm-tree-dotted beach. Little Courtney played in the gentle surf along with two other little girls, while Chris, Liza and Sam sat only several feet away.

"Eventually, you're going to have to tell Kyle that you can't go," said Chris. "You might as well get it over with."

"I'm not telling him," said Sam, digging her heels into the sand stubbornly. "It's not fair. I should be allowed to go. If it wasn't for Greta and dumb old Lloyd I wouldn't have this problem."

"Oh, that reminds me," said Chris. "I meant to tell you. I was talking to Julie, you know, the head lifeguard

77

here, and she said there's a job open as assistant pool manager."

"What happened to Joey?" asked Liza. "Did Julie fire him?"

"No, he decided to go to college," Chris explained. "Anyway, I thought it might be a perfect job for Lloyd."

"Forget it!" cried Sam.

"Why not?" asked Chris. "At least Lloyd would be outside and around water. It would be a job he wouldn't totally hate."

"I couldn't stand seeing Lloyd all the time!" cried Sam. "He would tell everyone that we know each other. I'd be embarrassed by every stupid thing he did! Sooner or later he's going to be back at my house. I know it. Then I'd have to see him at home *and* at work. There'd be no escaping him!"

"Okay, okay. Calm down," said Chris. "It was just a suggestion."

"I'm sorry," said Sam. "But the subject of Lloyd gets me mad. I don't want to talk about him anymore. I want to talk about this party and how I'm going to get there. Because I *am* going, no matter what!"

"Boy," said Liza. "I've never seen you so set on anything before."

"Yeah, well, maybe I'm finally growing up," Sam replied. "I'm thinking for myself."

"I don't know if defying your father is the way to go," said Chris as she drew hearts in the wet sand.

"What if your parents said you couldn't date Bruce?" Sam challenged. "What would you do?"

The water swept in, wiping out Chris's hearts. "I don't know. It would be horrible. But it's different—I'm madly in love with Bruce. Do you feel that way about Kyle?"

Sam looked away, out to the water. "That's not the point," she replied. "The point is that it's unfair for my father to forbid me to go out."

"If you say so," said Chris, beginning a new series of sand hearts.

"Sam! Sam! Look at me!" cried Courtney. The girls looked and saw that Courtney had caked wet sand around her braids until they stuck out of her head like lopsided Martian antennae. The two other little girls stood giggling behind Courtney. "I'm a space monster!" she called, curling her fingers into claws and baring her small white teeth.

Chris, Sam and Liza laughed at the silly sight. "Try explaining that one to Mrs. Rutherford," Liza giggled. "'Sorry that Courtney's hair is matted with sand. She thought she was a Martian.'"

Sam shook her head with an amused but exasperated air. "You have to watch that kid every second or she's up to something." Sam got up and slogged through the water. "Come on, Courtney," she said. "Let me wash some of that out."

"No! No!" screamed Courtney. "I like it this way."

Sam thought fast. "Want me to teach you to float?" she asked.

"Yeah!" Courtney shouted.

Sam supported Courtney as she lay on the top of the water, her eyes shut tight. The water took some of the sand from her hair. "It's easier to float without sand in your hair," Sam fibbed. "Can I wash some out?"

"All right," Courtney agreed. Still holding Courtney's bottom, Sam used her free hand to rub the gritty sand from Courtney's braids.

"That's better," she told Courtney. "Now relax and let the water hold you up."

At the end of the lesson, Courtney had floated on her own for a full minute. The little girl was ecstatic. "I floated! I floated!" she cried, skipping out of the water.

When their shift was over, the girls herded their kids back up to the lobby. Mrs. Rutherford, looking very blond and elegant in a white linen pants suit, came to get her daughter. "I floated, Mommy!" Courtney yelled as she ran to greet her mother.

Mrs. Rutherford smiled. "She always has such a good time with you, Sam."

"I'm glad," Sam answered.

"By any chance, would you be free to baby-sit for her tonight?" asked Mrs. Rutherford. "My husband and I were invited to a friend's for dinner. I said that we could only come if you were available. She's usually asleep by seven-thirty, but I would be uneasy leaving her with anyone else."

"The hotel doesn't offer sitting after five," Sam said.

"That's all right. I'll pay you directly. How does eight dollars an hour sound?"

Eight dollars an hour! thought Sam. *That's great!* But tonight she was going to the party at Kyle's. "I'm sorry, Mrs. Rutherford, I won't be able to, I have—"

Then a brilliant idea came to Sam.

"Oh, wait a minute," she said. "I can do it. I made a mistake. What time do you want me here?"

"Is seven okay?"

"Seven is fine. I'll be here," Sam answered.

"Terrific," said Mrs. Rutherford, taking Courtney's hand. "I'm so glad you're free to sit for her."

Chris and Liza had come up behind Sam and heard the last part of the conversation. "You're sitting for her tonight?" asked Liza.

"Good," added Liza. "I'm glad you decided not to go to that party."

Sam gave her friends a knowing smile. "Oh, I'm going to that party, all right."

"Wait a minute," said Chris confused. "How are you going to go to the party *and* take care of Courtney at the same time?"

"I'm not," said Sam. "One of you is going to sit for Courtney."

"Oh, no," said Chris, folding her arms.

"Are you crazy?" cried Liza.

"Come on, please, please, please, you have to," Sam begged. "Don't you see? It's a perfect plan. I'll come and stay with Courtney until the Rutherfords leave. Then you guys will mind Courtney until I come back from the party."

"Don't you think Courtney will say something to her parents?" Liza questioned.

"Her mother says she goes to bed at seven-thirty," Sam told them. "I'll have Kyle pick me up here at quarter to eight. Courtney will never know I was gone."

"I don't know," said Chris. "It sounds too risky."

"What could go wrong?" asked Sam. "Besides, she's paying eight dollars an hour."

"Wow!" said Liza. "That's a lot." She looked at Chris. "I'll do it, if you come with me. I don't want to be stuck with that kid all by myself if she wakes up."

Chris considered this. "Even if we split the money, it's as much as we'd make on a regular sitting job. And I did want to buy something new to wear Saturday . . ."

"Pretty, pretty please," Sam coaxed. "I'm always doing stuff that you guys ask me to do. I never, ever ask you to do anything."

"That is true," Liza admitted. "You're usually the sensible one, and *we* get *you* into trouble."

"That's right," Sam pressed. "And you won't even get into trouble."

"I'll do it if you'll do it," Chris said to Liza.

"Okay," Liza gave in. "I guess I owe it to you, Sam."

Sam gave a small whoop of delight. "All right! Thank you! You two are the best friends in the world. Now I have to go right home so I can change and be back by seven. You don't have to get here till seven-thirty. She'll be asleep. All you'll have to do is sit around, watch TV and drink sodas. It'll be a snap."

"I hope so," said Chris. "I still don't feel right about this."

"Don't worry," said Sam. "What could possibly go wrong?"

Chapter Thirteen

Sam's nerves were on edge as she walked through her front door. She wasn't used to sneaking anything past her parents. On the whole, she had always been a fairly law-abiding child. This was a first for her, and she was sure deceit was written in large letters across her forehead.

But Sam got mad all over again when she thought of how unreasonable her father was being. Why shouldn't she be allowed to date? Chris and Liza could.

"Hi," her mother called from the kitchen.

"Oh, hi, Mom," Sam answered, coming into the kitchen. "How's your headache today?"

Mrs. O'Neill laughed wearily as she stacked plates into the dishwasher. "It's gone. Greta and your father have called a cease-fire. It seems Lloyd has a job."

Sam's jaw dropped. "You're joking."

"No joke," chirped Greta, bouncing into the kitchen, still wearing the white cotton suit she'd worn to work.

"Lloyd called me at the office and told me today. Guess what it is."

"Sorry, Greta," said Sam, closing her eyes. "I'm trying to picture Lloyd at a job and absolutely no picture is coming into my head."

"He's the maître d' at a new seafood restaurant outside town called *La Maison Jacques*," Greta said proudly.

"Sounds fancy," commented Mrs. O'Neill.

"Doesn't it!" Greta sighed. "Daddy says he'll believe it when he sees it, so Lloyd is stopping over tonight before work."

"He's not coming over too late or anything, is he?" asked Sam, sounding worried.

"He'll be here any minute," said Greta. "Why?"

Sam tried hard to sound casual. "Oh, I was hoping you or Dad could drive me back to the hotel by seven. I have a baby-sitting job tonight."

"Tonight!" exclaimed Mrs. O'Neill. "How were you planning to get home?"

Sam winced. "I hadn't really thought about it."

"Don't look at me," said Greta. "Lloyd is using my car to go to work."

"I'll drive you," said Mr. O'Neill, coming into the kitchen.

"Thank you," Sam said in the cool, prim voice she'd been using to address her father ever since he'd forbidden her to date.

"You're welcome," he answered in a similar tone. Sam eyed him suspiciously. Was he making fun of her? She didn't have time to worry about it.

"I have to get ready for my, uh, job," she said, again feeling that she was lying badly. As she headed out of the kitchen and across the living room, there was a knock on the front door. Greta flew past Sam and pulled the door open.

"Oh, Lloyd!" she cried ecstatically. "You look—you look—gorgeous!"

Sam blinked at the sight of Lloyd. He stood in the living room wearing a tuxedo. His floppy, white-blond hair was combed back and gelled flat to his head. "Lloyd," said Sam. "I've never seen you so covered up."

Lloyd proudly ran his fingers down his lapels. "Pretty sophisticated, huh?"

"How handsome you look," said Mrs. O'Neill, coming out of the kitchen.

"Yes, well, they demand perfect groomingness at *La Maison Jacques*," Lloyd informed her.

"Coming over in a monkey suit doesn't exactly prove you have a job," said Mr. O'Neill skeptically.

Lloyd dug into the pocket of his black pants and pulled out a slip of paper. "But this does," he said, handing the slip to Mr. O'Neill.

"It's an income tax withholding form, all right," Mr. O'Neill had to admit.

Lloyd took the slip back from Mr. O'Neill. He snapped it once before putting it back into his pocket. "I am now a taxpaying, tip-collecting member of the working class. Now, if you'll all excuse me, my customers await me." With a smart salute, Lloyd turned and walked out the door.

"See, Daddy," said Greta. "It took Lloyd less than a week."

"Okay, now let's see how long he keeps this—" Mr. O'Neill was cut off by Lloyd's return.

"I need the keys to your car," he told Greta with a sheepish grin.

"Oh, right," said Greta. She dug them from the bottom of her straw handbag. "I'll walk you to the car," she told him.

Sam checked her watch. It was six-thirty. "I have to get out of here!" she cried, running up to her room. She stood in front of her bedroom closet and stared at the clothing. *What should I wear? What should I wear?* she repeated nervously.

She grabbed a blue cotton dress with a dropped waist. As she was buttoning it up the front, she stopped. Did it look too fancy to wear baby-sitting? Would it make her parents suspect that she wasn't really baby-sitting?

It will, she decided, quickly unbuttoning the dress and stepping out of it. Rummaging in her closet, she found a large plastic bag. She stuffed the dress into the bag and put on jeans and a T-shirt. Since this was a private sitting job, she didn't need to wear her official Palm Pavilion polo shirt.

I'll get ready at the hotel, she decided. The important thing now was simply to get there.

Makeup, she said, looking at the small tubes and bottles sitting in a jumble on top of Greta's dresser. *I should wear some makeup*. Sam picked out a lipstick, some blush and a mascara from Greta's things. She'd put it all back. Greta wouldn't mind.

With her makeup and dress in the bag, she bounded down the stairs. "I'm late, can we go now, Dad?" she said eagerly.

"Let's go," said her father, getting up from the couch.

It took only ten minutes by car to get to the hotel. As they drove along in Mr. O'Neill's blue van, Sam felt horribly uncomfortable. Even though she was angry at him, Sam had never lied to her father before, not about anything that mattered, anyway. And here he was being so nice and driving her to the hotel. It made Sam feel even worse.

I'm not really doing anything bad, Sam consoled herself. *If he wasn't so pigheaded I wouldn't have to lie to him.*

"Call me when you're ready to come home," he said, dropping her off in front of the hotel.

"Okay," said Sam as she climbed out of the van.

She had never seen the Palm Pavilion at night. Each palm tree that lined the long front drive was lit with its own spotlight. The canopied entrance was brilliantly illuminated with golden lights. Cabs pulled up and lavishly dressed men and women climbed inside. Sam couldn't imagine where they were driving off to. There wasn't a lot to do in Bonita Beach at night. They were probably heading for clubs and restaurants outside of town.

Feeling slightly scruffy in her jeans, she climbed the stairs of the main entrance. She was just inside the lobby when she saw Mr. Parker heading toward her. He wore a blue sports jacket and light blue seersucker pants. Sam had never seen him out of his usual day wear of shorts and sandals. "Miss O'Neill, what are you doing here at this hour?" he asked.

"Sitting for the Rutherfords," she told him.

Mr. Parker raised an eyebrow. "They are aware that the hotel has nothing to do with this?"

"I told them."

"Good," he said. "Be sure to comport yourself well. You are still an employee of the Palm—on duty or off—never forget that."

"I won't," she assured him. As she spoke, she felt guilty all over again. Mr. Parker was a pain, but there was something that Sam liked about him. For some reason, she wanted him to think well of her.

"I am heading out for the evening," he said with a polite nod. "I wish you a safe and enjoyable good evening."

"Same to you," Sam said. The minute he left, Sam raced for the elevator. It was several minutes after seven by the time she knocked on the Rutherfords' hotel door.

Courtney answered, dressed in a cotton nightgown, her long dark hair hanging loose past her shoulders. "Hi," she greeted Sam with a smile.

The Rutherfords gave Sam the phone number where they'd be and told her to order anything she wanted from room service. "We'll be home around midnight," Mrs. Rutherford told Sam as she kissed Courtney good night.

As soon as the couple left, Sam flew into action. First she called Kyle. "Why did you wait so long to call?" Kyle asked irritably.

"Sorry," said Sam. "Pick me up at the Palm, okay? Meet me in the lobby."

"I'll be right there," he said. "Everyone's dying to meet you."

"Terrific," Sam muttered as she put down the phone. All she needed was a roomful of people dying to meet her.

Next she changed. "Why are you putting on a dress?" Courtney asked.

"So I can look nice," Sam answered. She pulled down the covers of one of the two queen-sized beds. "Aren't you tired, Courtney?"

"No," she answered.

Sam scooped the girl up and sat her on the bed. She snapped on the TV. "Here, watch some TV. That will make you sleepy."

"But I don't want to be sleepy," Courtney objected.

"Sure you do," said Sam, leaning into the mirror and putting on Greta's makeup. "You've had a long day. You're very tired."

At seven-thirty Chris and Liza knocked on the door. "Hi, Courtney," Chris greeted the little girl.

"I thought she was going to be asleep!" Liza hissed.

"She will be, soon," said Sam nervously.

"What do we do if she doesn't go to sleep?" asked Chris.

Sam thought a moment. "I know." She turned to

Courtney. "I'm going downstairs for a moment, Courtney. Liza and Chris will stay with you until I come back."

Courtney frowned at the girls. "You better come back," she said.

"Of course I'm coming back," said Sam. "Here's the plan," she whispered to Chris and Liza, pulling them into the bathroom. "She'll fall asleep soon, and she'll never know I didn't come back right away. Her parents are due back at midnight. I'll come back at ten-thirty, eleven at the latest."

"You better come back in time," Chris said fretfully.

"I will, don't worry," said Sam. She stepped back from them and smiled. "How do I look?"

"Great," said Liza. "Except, do you really think those sneakers go with the dress?"

Sam looked down at her feet. She was wearing her white sneakers. "My sandals!" she cried. "I forgot to bring my sandals!"

Chapter Fourteen

"Hi, Kyle," said Sam, trying hard to smile. It wasn't easy, not with her size-seven feet stuck into Liza's size-six huarache sandals.

"Hi," he replied. "You look nice." They stood in the lobby of the Palm Pavilion. Sam thought that Kyle looked especially nice, himself. He wore a lemon-yellow cotton sweater over baggy, pleated tan pants.

There was a low whistle behind Sam. It was Raoul Smith, the bartender from the Parrot Lounge upstairs. "Looking pretty spiffy tonight, O'Neill," he complimented her.

Sam couldn't control the blush that swept across her face. "Thank you," she said as he went up the stairs, three wine bottles tucked under his arms.

"Come on," said Kyle, taking Sam's arm. "I don't want that guy to steal you away from me."

"Raoul!" Sam laughed. "Not likely. He's got to be in his thirties."

"I'm not taking any chances," said Kyle as they left through the front entrance. Despite her scrunched toes, Sam felt like Cinderella going to the ball.

Kyle had parked his father's white Buick off to the side. "Hop in," said Kyle. "The party has already started."

Sam got in on the passenger side. "Don't sit all the way over there," said Kyle, climbing in behind the wheel. "Come closer to me."

She slid over and Kyle put his arm around her. He held her tight and kissed her. Sam felt herself tense up.

"Relax," he said. "What's the matter?"

"Nothing," said Sam. "I don't want to be late, that's all."

"I thought maybe you didn't like kissing," he said sourly.

"Oh, no, kissing is fine," she replied with a nervous laugh. She inched away from him a little as he started the engine. *What's wrong with you?* she scolded herself. *Do you want him to think you're a complete child?* She promised herself to be more relaxed the next time he kissed her.

It took only fifteen minutes to get to Kyle's house. It was a white stucco house, slightly bigger than the average Bonita Beach house, thanks to a larger additional room that had been built off to the side. Cars lined the driveway and the street. Sam could hear music as they headed up the walkway. The party was obviously in full swing.

When they came into the front hall, Kyle called to a

petite woman with short white hair. She stood talking to a group of guests in the living room. "Mom, I want you to meet someone," he said.

Mrs. Jameson turned and smiled at her son. When she saw Sam, her eyes lit with recognition. She held out her arms and stepped toward them. "Why, Marianne, I—" she began. Then she stopped short, covering her mouth with her hand.

"Mother, wear your glasses," Kyle said in surly tone. "This isn't Marianne."

"Yes, I can see that now," said Mrs. Jameson. "Do forgive me, dear. It's just that at first glance the resemblance is so striking. I do apologize."

"That's all right," said Sam. "I'm Sam O'Neill."

"Samantha," Kyle corrected.

"Kyle likes my full name better," Sam explained awkwardly.

"Yes, well, whatever," said Mrs. Jameson. In the same way that Kyle had stared at Sam when they first met, Mrs. Jameson seemed unable to stop looking at Sam. Self-conscious, Sam smoothed her hair.

"Kyle, introduce your friend to our guests," his mother said. "I must get my quiches from the oven."

"Who is Marianne?" Sam asked as Mrs. Jameson scurried off toward the kitchen.

"Nobody," he replied. "Come on, I see my father over there." He took Sam's arm and guided her through the crowded living room to a bald-headed man with a large, protruding belly. He stood at a table fixing himself a drink. Sam was immediately struck by the fact that he and Kyle had almost the same face. *Is that what Kyle will look like someday?* she wondered. She looked up at Kyle's strong jaw and tried to picture it fat and jowly like his father's. Yes, it was the same face, all right.

"Dad, this is Samantha," Kyle introduced her.

Mr. Jameson took her hand. Sam didn't like the feel of it. She'd never known a man to have such a smooth, soft hand. "My, my," he said, a twinkle in his watery blue eyes. "It's nice to meet you."

"You, too," Sam replied politely. She realized from the look in his eyes that he'd already had a few too many drinks that evening. Sam tried to take her hand back, but he held on.

"I guess we know that this girl is your type, eh, Kyle?" said Mr. Jameson. Sam didn't like the tone of his voice. It was as though this was some private joke she wasn't in on.

"I don't know what you mean, Dad," Kyle said irritably.

Mr. Jameson chuckled. "A bit on the Marianne-ish side, don't you think?"

"No, I don't," said Kyle.

At that moment Mrs. Jameson called to her son, "Kyle, come help me in the kitchen a moment."

"I'll be right back," said Kyle, running off to the kitchen.

One of the guests joined Mr. Jameson. Sam stood there, not knowing what to do next. Mr. Jameson started talking to the man about insurance premiums, barely noticing her.

"Excuse me," Sam said in a small voice.

"Oh, yes, nice to meet you," Mr. Jameson said quickly.

Sam wandered over to the food table. She began serving herself some ziti and salad. "Marianne, how nice to see you," said a very small woman with tight gray curls.

"I'm not Marianne," said Sam. "Though everyone seems to think I look just like her."

The woman stepped back and studied Sam. "You're a dead ringer. Why, Marianne even wore her hair back in a ponytail just like yours. Pardon me, I'm Kyle's great-aunt, Viola."

"I'm Sam," she introduced herself. "Who is Marianne, anyway?"

"Marianne was Kyle's girlfriend from the time they were both thirteen. Those two did everything together." Aunt Viola moved closer to Sam. Her voice took on a secretive, confidential tone. "When the family moved, Kyle wanted to still have a long-distance romance, but Marianne said no. She wanted to date other people. She said Kyle was smothering her. That's what my niece, Kyle's mother, told me. She heard them talking over the phone late one night." Aunt Viola looked at Sam for a reaction.

"That's, um, too bad," Sam said.

"It certainly is," Aunt Viola agreed. "His mother said Kyle was heartbroken. I don't understand girls today. I'd think a girl would be thrilled to have a boy like Kyle. Smothering her! Who ever heard of such a thing?"

"Yes, I suppose," said Sam, not knowing how to reply.

As Kyle's great-aunt began piling food on her plate, Sam tried to absorb all that the old woman had said. That explained it all! Kyle didn't like her—not for herself, anyway. He was pretending he was back with his old girlfriend!

The realization hit Sam like a punch in the stomach. She held onto the table for support. "You're quite pale, hon," said Aunt Viola. "I hope I haven't upset you."

"No, I'm okay," Sam muttered. "Please, excuse me." She had to get away from all these people. She needed air.

Sam hurried through the guests, heading for the front door. On her way, Mrs. Jameson stopped her. "There's a phone call for you, Samantha," she said. "You can take it in the kitchen."

"For me?" said Sam, surprised. "Who could be calling—" Then she realized that the only ones who knew where she was were Chris and Liza!

She hurried to the kitchen and picked up the phone. "Hello," she said anxiously.

Sam recognized Liza's voice immediately. "I'm sorry, Sam," she said. "But you just have to get back here. Courtney has been screaming since you left. We've tried everything!"

"All right," said Sam. "I'm on my way."

As she hung up, Kyle came in the kitchen door holding a large bag of ice. "I had to go get ice for Mom. Now we can—" He stopped when he saw Sam's stricken expression.

"I have to leave, Kyle," said Sam. "Right now!"

Chapter Fifteen

Sam clutched her hands together tightly as Kyle pulled the car out of his driveway. "I don't know where you live," he said.

"Oh, um, I have to go to the Palm," she told him.

"Why do you want to go there?"

"Oh, Kyle," she said. "I might as well tell you the truth." She explained everything to him—about how she was forbidden to date, and the scheme she'd concocted with Liza and Chris.

He seemed pleased as he listened to her words. "I guess you really do like me," he commented. "You went through a lot to be with me tonight."

Sam considered this, and she suddenly knew very clearly that it wasn't true. She didn't like him all that much. She'd never felt comfortable around him. Not for one moment. All she'd wanted was a boyfriend. She'd plotted and schemed so that she wouldn't lose her boyfriend—not Kyle in particular. It could have been anyone.

It didn't make her feel proud of herself. But she'd been lying to herself as much as to Kyle. She hadn't meant to hurt him.

And what about Kyle? He didn't care about her. He only wanted a Marianne look-alike. No wonder he had been so enthralled with her right from the start!

"Did you realize that I look like your old girlfriend?" she asked Kyle.

He turned to her with a startled expression. "Who told you about Marianne?"

"Aunt Viola."

"Aunt Viola is senile," he said angrily. "Marianne doesn't look anything like you."

Sam knew he was lying. His mother and father had also said she looked like Marianne.

Suddenly Sam realized she didn't know where they were. "This isn't the way to the Palm," she said. They had turned down a dark road. Several small houses were set back behind thick foliage. There were only a few streetlights, set a good distance apart. Kyle pulled the car over into a dark spot.

"Why are we stopping here?" asked Sam.

Kyle leaned forward and put his arm around her. "I thought we could have a few moments of privacy before I take you back," he said.

"I can't," she told him urgently. "I left Liza and Chris in a bad spot. Courtney is hard to control."

"They've handled it this long," he said smoothly. "They can hold out a little longer."

He tried to draw her to him, but she pulled back. "Kyle, I have to go!" she shouted.

Kyle let her go. He slapped the steering wheel with his palm. "I don't get you. You go through all this to go out with me tonight. Then you turn cold on me. What's with you?"

"We're not right for each other," Sam blurted out. "I was flattered that you liked me—but you don't even like me for *me*, Kyle! I just remind you of Marianne."

"So, what if you do?" Kyle argued. "Is that a big sin?"

"I guess not, but it means you don't care for *me*," said Sam. "Look, I'm to blame, too. I thought it would be nice to have you for a boyfriend. Maybe I wasn't seeing the real you, either."

Kyle slid his arm around the back of the seat. "Let's get to know each other, then," he said in a sultry voice.

"I really do have to go," Sam insisted.

"Fine!" Kyle snarled, turning the ignition back on. "That's what I get for dating an infant!"

"Sorry I'm not Marianne," Sam snapped back at him.

"You know what? I am, too. Marianne knew how to have a good time. You only look like Marianne, but you're nowhere near as good as she was."

"Is that so?" yelled Sam. "Let me tell you something . . ." Sam tried to think of something snappy to say, but nothing came to her. She was too upset. All she wanted to do was get away from him. She opened the car door and started to get out.

"What do you think you're doing?" he said. "Get in and I'll drop you at the Palm."

Sam realized that she didn't have much choice. Sullenly, she climbed back in. Kyle pulled the car onto the road and began to drive.

"You're still going the wrong way," she informed him stiffly.

"I know a short cut," he said.

After they drove for a while, Sam began to feel badly. Maybe she *had* led him on. Maybe she was acting babyish. "Kyle, I'm sorry," she said. "I was just so shocked to find out about Marianne."

"Are you really sorry?" he asked, looking at her from the corner of his eye.

"Yes, I may have overreacted."

"I was hoping you'd feel that way," said Kyle, pulling over to the side of the road again. The next thing Sam knew, Kyle was holding her tight and kissing her.

"Kyle, stop," she said.

"I don't think you really mean it," Kyle said breathlessly.

"Yes, Kyle," Sam said, shoving him hard. "I *do* mean it." Quickly she jumped out of the car.

"Get in," he ordered her, annoyed.

"No thanks, Kyle. I'd rather call someone to come get me," she said through the window.

"Suit yourself," Kyle shouted.

Sam jumped back as Kyle stepped on the gas and zoomed away down the road. Her eyes filled with tears. She wasn't sorry to see him go; she was just so upset.

Suddenly she was extremely aware of how much her feet hurt. She was sure a blister was forming on her left heel. *I'll stick a tissue between the blister and the sandal*, she decided.

That's when she realized that she didn't have her pocketbook. She'd left it in Kyle's car.

"I don't believe this," she moaned. A breeze whistled through the dark leaves behind her. In the distance were a few houses, but she felt shy about approaching them.

Sam knew she was several miles outside of town. She wasn't sure where she was. She could head back in the direction they'd come, but they hadn't passed a store or a phone booth for a long time. Maybe she would do better heading in the opposite direction. If she could find a store, surely someone would give her the money for a phone call.

She trudged on down the dark road. A breeze was coming up and clouds blocked the moon, making the road seem pitch-black in spots. Her feet were hurting more and more. Every step she took was an agony.

This has got to be the worst night of my life, she thought as she stooped to take off her sandals. *I can't imagine how it could be any worse.*

Just then, a fat raindrop hit Sam squarely on the nose.

Chapter Sixteen

Sam bent her head against the hard rain and continued down the dark road. "Ouch!" she cried as her bare feet come down on a sharp rock. The only thing that was keeping her going was the sight of a tiny, flashing pink light off in the distance.

As she neared the light, she saw it was part of a neon sign. *Where there's a big sign, there's usually a public phone,* she figured. Her plan was to call someone collect—although she wasn't quite sure yet who that someone should be.

It took her another ten minutes to reach the sign. Finally, though, she came to a large dirt parking lot packed with cars. Through the driving rain she was finally able to read the sign. The words "Jack's Crab Shack" blinked on and off atop a low, shingled building.

"Oh, yuck," Sam muttered as she squished her way across the muddy parking lot. She leaned against a car to put Liza's sandals back on. "Ooooow, forget it," she groaned, discovering that she'd formed not one, but two blisters on her heel.

When Sam looked up from her feet, she saw something that made her heart beat with joy. There, bathed in the pink light of the neon sign, was Greta's old, beat-up blue Mustang.

That's got to be it, thought Sam, hurrying to the car. *The dents seem to be in all the right places.* Sure enough, Sam caught sight of Greta's window decal that read: LIFE'S A BEACH.

Boy, am I lucky, thought Sam gratefully. *Greta will take me back to the Palm.*

Then Sam realized something. *Lloyd took Greta's car tonight.* But he was supposed to be at his new job tonight. Sam looked up at the blinking sign. *La Maison Jacques—Jack's Crab Shack.* "Very funny, Lloyd," she said out loud. This was obviously the place where Lloyd worked. He had dressed up the name, probably to impress Mr. O'Neill.

Sam headed for the front door. There was no sense running; she was already soaked to the skin. It would have been impossible to get any wetter.

She hesitated at the front door. What would they think when she entered, sopping wet, her feet caked with mud? But her only other choice was to keep walking up the road—and there was no way she was going to do that.

Wincing with pain, Sam stuffed her feet into Liza's sandals. "Here goes," she said, pushing on the heavy wooden door. Immediately she was greeted by an almost deafening din. No one took any notice of her at all, as waiters and waitresses rushed by with huge trays of steaming crabs balanced on their shoulders. Customers sat at long wooden tables. They smashed the crabs right on the table using wooden mallets. Everyone seemed to be talking loudly as they ate crabs and washed them down with pitchers of beer or soda.

A short man wearing a bright yellow-and-pink shirt greeted her at the door. The word "Jack's" was emblazoned across his right pocket. "Can I do something for you?" he asked Sam.

"I, uh, need to speak to the maître d'," Sam said timidly.

The man barked out a hoarse laugh. "The what?" he said, chuckling.

"The maître d'," Sam repeated.

"I heard you," the man said with a laugh. "Does this look like the kind of place that would have a maître d'?"

"Oh, well, does someone named Lloyd work here?" she asked, feeling extremely foolish.

"You mean the new guy over there?" said the man. He pointed across the room to where Lloyd stood. He was wearing the same yellow-and-pink shirt as the man at the door wore. His slicked-back hair now stood out at odd points, and the expression on his face was one of total confusion as he waved a tray of crabs above his head.

"Over here!" Sam heard a man yell to Lloyd from one of the tables.

Lloyd turned quickly and banged into the table nearest him. The tray flew from his hands.

Sam cringed as the crabs slid down onto the people seated at the table. Apologetically, Lloyd lifted one off a woman's teased blond hairdo. After Lloyd had scooped up the rest of the crabs, he signaled to the other table to wait a moment.

"Yes, that's him," Sam told the man.

"Uh-huh," said the man dryly. "Somehow it doesn't surprise me that you two go together."

"I'm his sister," Sam fibbed, feeling the need for some explanation. "I just have to ask him something."

"Your brother Lloyd there seems a little busy," said the man. "Can you wait a minute?"

"Sure," Sam replied. She stood there dripping onto the wooden floor while the man went over and spoke to Lloyd. She saw a look of surprise, then concern, come over Lloyd's face as the man spoke to him.

Immediately Lloyd laid down the armful of crabs he'd just dropped and hurried over to Sam. "Are you okay?" he asked.

"I've been better," said Sam. "But I'm not hurt or anything."

"You're sure?" said Lloyd.

"Yeah, I'm okay," Sam assured him. "It's a long story. Could you lend me money to take a cab to the Palm? It's probably not more than five dollars."

Lloyd fished in his pocket and came up with four crumpled singles and a handful of change. "And here's a dollar more for the phone," he said, counting out the coins. "After that, I'm tapped out."

He guided her through the crowd to a public phone booth near the bar. "Hey, Lloyd," called a waiter, rushing past. "Table five needs a pitcher of root beer. And table six is still waiting for those crabs you dumped on table three."

"Okay, okay, I got a family emergency here," Lloyd called back.

Sam looked at Lloyd gratefully. She really owed him for this.

Luckily the numbers of three different cab services were tacked up next to the phone. The first service Sam dialed had no cars available for over an hour. "When it rains, everyone needs a cab," the man at the cab service told her.

Before Sam could try the next service, Lloyd rapped on the glass door of the booth. He held his black tuxedo jacket out to her. "Here, put this on," he said as she slid open the door. "Be careful with it, though. I have to return it to the rental place on Monday."

"You mean you rented this just to—" Sam began.

"Lloyd, table five needs you," a waiter cut her off.

"Be right back," Lloyd told her.

Sam tried the other two cab companies. Neither of them could tell her when they'd have a cab available. She checked her watch. It was five after ten. She wondered what was going on with Courtney. Would Liza and Chris ever speak to her again?

"Any luck?" asked Lloyd, coming back to the booth.

"No," Sam said miserably.

"How did you get into this mess, anyway?" Lloyd asked.

As quickly as she could, Sam explained what had happened. ". . . so, I got out of the car and Kyle drove off," she concluded her story.

"What a creep!" Lloyd actually sounded angry.

"I know," Sam said. "But now I have to get back to the Palm because Courtney is screaming. At this rate, I won't even get there before the Rutherfords come home. What am I going to do?"

"Hang on a second," said Lloyd. "I'll be right back."

While he was gone Sam phoned the Palm Pavilion and asked for the Rutherfords' room. The phone rang and rang. "Sorry, no one is picking up," the hotel operator came back on the line. "Do you care to leave a message?"

"No. No message," said Sam. Where could they have gone? Had something awful happened to Courtney?

Sam slumped down into the seat of the phone booth. It was completely hopeless. In one night she had managed to lose a boyfriend, and possibly her two best friends. She would probably lose her job if Mr. Parker found out about this. And she didn't even want to think about what would happen if her parents found out.

"Okay, come on," said Lloyd, returning to the phone booth.

"Where?" asked Sam.

"My boss said I could leave for a half-hour," said Lloyd. "I'll drive you to the Palm."

Sam threw her arms around Lloyd. "Thank you, Lloyd. Thank you! Thank you! Thank you!"

"You're welcome," said Lloyd. "But do you mind not hugging me? You're kind of damp, if you know what I mean."

Sam jumped back. "Oh, sorry." She followed Lloyd out into the pouring rain. Holding his tuxedo jacket over her head, she ran for Greta's car.

"Here we go," said Lloyd, starting the engine. He flipped his white-blond hair out of his eyes, spraying Sam with rainwater. She'd seen him flip his hair back like that a million times. The gesture had always irked her. Suddenly it didn't bother her anymore. It just seemed like a very Lloyd-ish mannerism.

"I really appreciate this, Lloyd," she told him. "You don't know how much."

"Hey, what's family for?" he said, driving out of the parking lot.

"We're not really family, though," Sam pointed out.

"When Greta and I get married, you'll be my sister-in-law."

Lloyd's words jolted Sam. She'd hoped her father had put the marriage plans on hold. Now, it seemed, Lloyd was determined to go through with it. "Are you really going to get married?" Sam asked.

"Definitely," said Lloyd. "I mean, maybe not as soon as we'd planned. Your father is a hardnose, but he had a point. I didn't really realize how tough this working business is. It takes some getting used to. And Greta deserves a guy who can hold a job. That's the least she deserves. I see that now."

"That's good," said Sam, relieved to hear Lloyd making so much sense.

"I'm going to make good, though," said Lloyd as they drove down the dark road where Sam had been stranded. "I put Greta in a tough spot with your father, and I want to make it up to her. That's why I rented that tuxedo. I didn't want him to think I was just some crummy waiter in a crab joint. I wanted Greta to be proud."

They stopped at a red light. The pounding rain and the *Thwap! Thwap! Thwap!* of the wipers was the only sound. Sam looked at Lloyd's profile. His expression was serious, thoughtful. It was as if she were seeing him for the first time. All these years she'd treated him like some kind of joke. But she'd never seen this earnest side of Lloyd before. Nor had she noticed how decent and kind he really was. Though, she had to admit now, he had always been nice to her.

Maybe Lloyd was finally growing up. Maybe they both were.

"You really love Greta, don't you?" Sam observed as the light changed.

"Are you kidding?" said Lloyd. "Greta is the greatest. There's nothing I wouldn't do for her. I would die for Greta."

Sam put her hand on his shoulder. "I believe you."

They drove on without talking much more, until

finally the long, illuminated stretch of the Palm Pavilion's drive twinkled before them through the rain.

"Good luck," said Lloyd, stopping the car in front of the hotel.

Sam climbed out of the car. "Thanks."

She ran toward the front door. Some of the guests eyed her suspiciously. She knew she looked a wreck, but she couldn't worry about that now.

Sam raced through the lobby to the elevator. In a few minutes she was standing in front of the Rutherfords' room. She checked her watch. It was only ten to eleven. At least she'd made it back in time.

In a minute she heard the door being unlocked. "I made it," she said as the door began to open. "You don't know what I went through to—"

Sam stopped short.

Standing in front of her was Mrs. Rutherford.

Chapter Seventeen

Sam, Chris and Liza sat glumly on the velvet-covered bench of the Palm's fancy ladies' powder room. Sam leaned forward, her chin resting on her knuckles. Liza and Chris, exhausted, sat on either side of her, leaning against the back wall.

"I'm really sorry," Sam said, for what seemed like the hundredth time since her return.

"I should be furious at you," yawned Chris, "but I'm too tired."

"Me, too," agreed Liza, smearing her mascara as she rubbed her tired and bloodshot eyes. "Besides, you look like you've suffered enough."

"I have," Sam assured her, gingerly touching her blistered heel.

"And you really couldn't have predicted that Courtney would come down with the flu," added Chris. "We didn't want to call the Rutherfords. But once she started throwing up, we had to."

"Forget it, you did the right thing," said Sam. "I'm the one who messed everything up. I'm sorry you guys had such a terrible night."

Liza lifted herself off the bench. "We survived," she said. "But Mrs. Rutherford sure was furious when she saw you weren't there. Do you think she's going to tell Parker?"

"They're checking out early tomorrow," Sam said hopefully. "Maybe she won't see him before then." She shook her head wearily. "Gosh, was she ever mad! If looks could kill, I'd be dead right now."

Liza wandered over to the public telephone on the wall. "I'm going to call us a cab."

"You won't get one," Sam warned.

But the rain had stopped and Liza was able to get a cab company that promised to send a cab in a half-hour. Using their baby-sitting money, they had the cab drive them home.

"What are your parents going to say when they see you looking such a mess?" Chris asked as they pulled up in Sam's driveway.

"I don't know," she admitted. "I'll tell you tomorrow."

Sam's parents were up when she came in. "Honey, are you all right?" asked her mother, flying out of her chair at the sight of Sam. "Some boy named Kyle has been calling here every half-hour. He won't say what he wants, but he sounds upset. And you look terrible."

Mr. O'Neill turned off the TV. "What happened?" he asked seriously.

"Oh, I might as well tell you the truth!" Sam cried, too

weary to lie. "But you're not going to like it." She sat down on the couch and told them everything. The only part she left out was about Lloyd's job. She told them she'd found Lloyd working, just as he'd said, in a fancy restaurant as a maître d'. After all he'd done for her, she couldn't tell on him.

"And this Kyle," growled her father. "He didn't hurt you, did he?"

"No," Sam said. "Only my feelings. That's all."

"I never thought I'd say this," Mr. O'Neill grumbled. "But thank goodness for Lloyd."

"Yes, we've been too hard on the boy," said Mrs. O'Neill. "I wonder how he's doing without his jacket."

Sam took the black tuxedo jacket from her shoulders and hung it in the closet. "He said they had a spare," she told her parents.

"I haven't decided whether you've learned your lesson, or you deserve to be punished. I'll tell you in the morning," her father informed her.

"Dad," Sam said timidly. "Can I ask a favor?"

"What?"

"If you decide to punish me, could you find something besides grounding me? I really want to go to gymnastics practices. And I don't want to lose my job at the Palm."

Mr. O'Neill smiled for the first time since she'd come home. "I think that can be arranged," he said. "Now go to bed."

"Take a warm shower first," added her mother.

While Sam was showering, Greta knocked on the door. "Some guy named Kyle is on the phone for you," she told

Sam when she cracked open the door. "Mom and Dad went to bed, so you can get it in the kitchen."

Wrapped in her robe, Sam ventured downstairs through the dark house. Greta had left the phone off the hook and gone to their bedroom. "Hello," said Sam, picking up the phone.

"Samantha. I'm sorry about what happened. I had to make sure you got home all right," said Kyle.

"Don't worry about it, Kyle," said Sam. "I'm home now."

"Do you hate me?" asked Kyle.

"No," Sam answered. "But I don't think we're right for each other. It's not going to work out."

There was silence on the other end. "It might, if you could warm up a little," Kyle said after a moment. "We'll talk about it tomorrow. I'll see you at work."

Sam was suddenly very tired. Without another word, she hung up the phone. *Not if I see you first, Kyle*, she thought as she trudged up the stairs to bed.

The next morning, all Sam's muscles ached. She longed to sleep late, but she was due at work at ten. When she came down for breakfast, she was surprised to see Lloyd sitting with Greta at the kitchen table.

"I don't think you were meant to be a maître d'," Greta was saying sympathetically. "It wasn't the right kind of job for you, anyway."

"What happened?" asked Sam from the kitchen doorway.

"Lloyd got fired for driving you home," Greta told her pointedly.

"Really?" asked Sam sheepishly.

"Aw, no," said Lloyd, flipping his hair back casually. "Well, kind of. But that job wasn't for me, anyway." Lloyd got up from the table. "Anyway, I just came by to return the car and get my jacket. I have to return it to the rental . . . I mean, restaurant today."

"I'm sorry," Sam said while Greta went for the jacket. "I thought you said it was okay with your boss."

"I didn't want you to worry," he said.

Greta returned with the jacket. "You'll find a better job," she said.

"Yeah, well, I'd better get going before your father wakes up and finds me here," said Lloyd, heading for the door.

"Lloyd, wait," Sam said. "There's a job at the Palm. Assistant pool manager. It might be just right for you."

Lloyd's eyes lit up with interest. "Hey, that does sound good," he said eagerly. "Who do I see?"

"Julie the—" Sam got up from the table. "Hang on one second and I'll go with you and introduce you to her." Sam ran upstairs and dressed quickly. By the time she came downstairs, Chris and Liza were knocking on the front door.

"Are you ready to go see if we still have jobs?" said Chris.

Sam crossed her fingers. "I'll meet you there," she told them. "I'm going to drive in with Lloyd. He's applying for the pool job."

"Okay!" said Liza. "See you there."

Sam and Lloyd took Greta's car to work and arrived at

nine-thirty. The first person Sam saw when she stepped into the lobby was Mr. Parker. She froze as he headed toward her.

"Good morning, Miss O'Neill," he said approvingly. "Glad to see you here early, for a change."

"Thank you—I mean, you're welcome—I mean, no problem," Sam stammered.

Mr. Parker looked confused but kept walking.

Sam sighed with relief. It seemed she still had her job.

Sam hurried Lloyd out to the pool, and found Julie, the head lifeguard. Sam introduced her to Lloyd, and the two of them went to the far end of the pool to talk about the job.

As she headed back through the hotel lobby to punch her time card, Sam ran into Chris and Liza. "I just saw Parker," Sam told them, "and he didn't seem to know anything about last night."

Liza staggered back dramatically. "Thank heavens!"

"Guess who we just saw?" Chris said. "Kyle. He says you guys broke up last night."

"He wasn't for you," said Liza. "He had no sense of humor. And he was too stuck on himself."

"I'm glad, too," said Chris. "You deserve someone much better, not so pushy."

"Maybe," said Sam. "But now that still leaves me out when you guys double date."

"Chris and I were just talking," Liza told her. "We don't have to double date. We can go out on different nights. I mean, it's not like we have to see each other every second."

"And that way, one of us will be free to hang out with you when the other one is on a date. It'll be perfect," added Chris.

"I'm lucky to have you guys for friends," said Sam, touched by their offer.

Chris put her arm around Sam's shoulder. "You're right. You are," she teased.

Just then, Lloyd came hurrying toward them from across the lobby. "Well?" asked Sam.

"You are looking at the Palm Pavilion's new assistant pool manager," he said, fairly bursting with pride.

"Congratulations!" cried Chris.

"Yeah, cool!" seconded Liza.

"Thanks, Sam," said Lloyd. "Thanks a million."

Sam smiled at him. "Hey," she said, "that's what family is for."

SUZANNE WEYN

Suzanne Weyn is the author of many books for children and young adults. Among them are: *The Makeover Club*, *Makeover Summer* and the series NO WAY BALLET. Suzanne began baby-sitting at the age of thirteen. Later, while attending Harpur College, she worked as a waitress in a hotel restaurant. Suzanne grew up on Long Island, N.Y., and loves the beach. Sailing, snorkeling, water-skiing and swimming are some of her favorite activities. In SITTING PRETTY she is able to draw on these experiences.

Suzanne now has a baby of her own named Diana, who has two terrific baby sitters—Chris and Joy-Ann.